Praise

'*What It Was* is a vividly .... day Bonnie and Clyde account of two lovers on a murderous rampage . . . As aficionados of *The Wire* will attest, Pelecanos is a peerless chronicler of the black urban underclass and his book is rich in detail about fashion and music and American muscle cars . . . The author's skilful evocation of a crucial moment in American history as seen from the street, rather than a more historical account, is entertainingly rewarding' *Sunday Express*

'A sizzling flashback to the Watergate summer of 1972 . . . *What It Was* features plenty of tough talk, hot cars, hotter women and keenly crafted social and racial observation, all set to a pumping funk and soul soundtrack' *Irish News*

'A lean but lethal thriller . . . the world of muscle cars, teetering afros and scratchy soul records proves so intoxicating you'll devour it in one sitting' *Shortlist*

'*The Wire* writer George Pelecanos has a way with words that only seems to be getting meaner and swankier' *Mirror*

'A well-written potboiler about vicious criminals and virtuous investigators in seventies Washington DC . . . it's a mind-blowing trip' *Sunday Telegraph*

'Author of over 18 critically-lauded novels . . . his reputation rests on a bedrock of tight, fast-paced prose, meticulous plotting, finely tuned characters and an incredible authenticity in depicting time and place . . . *What It Was* does not disappoint. This is a writer in full control of his material and fully understanding of his strengths. Lovers of crime fiction should not miss what he has to say' *Irish Examiner*

'A complex tale of drug-dealing and detection in Washington DC . . . it manages to combine a fond trip down memory lane – dig those groovy clothes and classic hits – with an equally fond tribute to pulp noir' *Evening Standard*

By George Pelecanos

A Firing Offense
Nick's Trip
Shoedog
Down By the River Where the Dead Men Go
The Big Blowdown
King Suckerman
The Sweet Forever
Shame the Devil
Right as Rain
Hell to Pay
Soul Circus
Hard Revolution
Drama City
The Night Gardener
The Turnaround
The Way Home
The Cut
What It Was

George Pelecanos is an independent-film producer, an essayist, the recipient of numerous international writing awards, a producer and an Emmy-nominated writer on the HBO hit series *The Wire*, and the author of a bestselling series of novels set in and around Washington, D.C. He is currently a writer and producer for the acclaimed HBO series *Treme*. He lives in Maryland with his wife and three children.

WHAT IT WAS

GEORGE PELECANOS

An Orion paperback

First published in Great Britain in 2012
by Orion
This paperback edition published in 2012
by Orion Books,
an imprint of The Orion Publishing Group Ltd,
Orion House, 5 Upper St Martin's Lane,
London WC2H 9EA

An Hachette UK company

1 3 5 7 9 10 8 6 4 2

ISBN 978-1-4091-3950-8

Printed and bound in Great Britain by
Clays Ltd, St Ives plc

The Orion Publishing Group's policy is to use papers
that are natural, renewable and recyclable products and
made from wood grown in sustainable forests. The logging
and manufacturing processes are expected to conform to
the environmental regulations of the country of origin.

www.orionbooks.co.uk

AUTHOR'S NOTE

This novel came about serendipitously, as novels often do. Many years ago I was sitting in the offices of *The Wire*, bullshitting with my friend and partner, Ed Burns. Before becoming a television writer and producer, Ed, a combat veteran of Vietnam, had been a police officer, a homicide detective, and a public school teacher in Baltimore. He's lived a full life. Our discussion revolved around his experiences as a young patrolman in uniform, and the relationship between the police and the underworld in the 1970s. I'm guessing Ed does not even remember our talk that day, but I do. I was taking notes.

A couple of years later, I was looking through morgue material in the *Washington Post*, doing some halfhearted research for a possible Watergate novel that I had no great desire to write. In the library I came upon two articles: "5 Held in Plot to Bug Democrats' Office Here" and "Cadillac Smith's Legend of Violence." Both carried the byline of the *Post*'s revered longtime crime reporter Alfred E. Lewis. Sensing something I might use later on, I planted a fable within my novel *The Night Gardener* (2006) about a character named Red "Fury" Jones, very loosely based on the exploits of notorious D.C. criminal Raymond "Cadillac" Smith. It was a way of forcing my hand to eventually complete his story in a future novel. The idea was that someday I'd give Red his own book.

AUTHOR'S NOTE

As a result of a brief conversation I had with Ed Burns, and two newspaper articles written by Alfred E. Lewis, I had the ammunition to ignite my imagination. *What It Was*, the book you hold in your hand, was written in a fever in the summer of 2011.

MANY THANKS to Ed Burns and the late Alfred E. Lewis.

WHAT IT WAS

INTRO

JOHNNIE WALKER," said Derek Strange. "Rocks."

"Red or Black?" said the bartender. His name was Leonides Vazoulis, but folks on Georgia Avenue called him Leo. The short version was arranged horizontally, in neon, on the sign outside the bar.

"Make it the Black."

"How about you, *patrioti?*" said Leo, thick and bald, pointing to a fellow Greek who sat beside Strange. "Heineken?"

The Greek was middle-aged, thin, solidly built, with short hair salted gray. He wore 501s and a faded black T-shirt from the Harley store in Key West. On his feet were black high-top Chucks.

"Yeah," said Nick Stefanos. "And put a Knob Creek next to it. Neat."

Strange settled in, shifting his broad shoulders beneath his black leather blazer. His closely cropped hair was shaped up and correct. A Vandyke beard, straight silver against dark skin, framed his mouth. "Thought you were a Grand-Dad man."

"You moved up the shelf. So can I."

"I stopped with the Red when I turned sixty. If I'm gonna drink, I'm gonna enjoy every sip."

Leo served them. They tapped glasses and drank without comment. The silence was pleasant in the way that it can be between men. Plus, Bettye LaVette was singing "Your Turn to Cry" from the juke. Strange and Stefanos were showing respect.

When the song was done, Stefanos crossed the empty room and stopped at the jukebox, which was stocked with soul rarities, funk, and R&B singles. Strange wondered what Stefanos, a rock and punk man, would choose. Stefanos punched in some buttons and moved toward the head as a song began to play. Through the plate glass fronting Leo's, Strange watched a slanting downpour hit the street.

Boy went for theme music, thought Strange. And: *It's a good day to drink.*

" 'I wanna go outside…in the rain,' " sang Strange, very softly.

It got him to thinking on the year that song had hit the charts. And, as thoughts of the past did more often of late, this drove his mind further into a cinematic recollection of that thrilling time.

"Nice choice," said Strange, as Stefanos settled back onto his barstool.

"Call it."

"The Dramatics. Nineteen seventy-two."

"The summer Watergate broke."

"You ask some people on this side of town to recollect that year, they wouldn't think on Nixon. They're gonna tell you that seventy-two was the summer that Red went off."

"Red?"

"Some called him Red Fury."

Stefanos hit his bourbon and waited for the rest.

"Robert Lee Jones was his given name," said Strange. "He was known by Red from when he was a kid, on account of his light skin and the tint of his hair. Fury was the car his woman drove."

"So?"

"You're funny, man."

Strange put up two fingers and made a swirling motion over the empties that were parked on the mahogany. Leo commenced to pouring their next round of drinks.

"You were, what, twenty-five in seventy-two?"

"That summer? I was twenty-six. But this ain't about me."

"We got all afternoon," said Stefanos.

"Then let me tell it," said Strange.

ONE

IT WAS a Plymouth Fury, the GT Sport, a two-door 440 V-8 with hidden headlamps and a four-barrel carb. The color scheme was red over white, and its vanity plates read "Coco." White interior made it a woman's car. The bright finish and the personalized tags would render the vehicle easily identifiable around town, but Robert Lee Jones was unconcerned. To him it was important that he be remembered and that what he did got done with style.

Jones had bought the Fury for his woman, Coco Watkins, whose Christian name was Shirley. She was in the wheel bucket of the Plymouth, a Viceroy in her long-nailed hand resting atop the driver's-side mirror. She and Jones were idling in park, facing south on 13th, between S and R, in Northwest. The in-dash radio was set on 1450. A Betty Wright number was playing.

Coco, so nicknamed because of the dark, buttery texture of her skin, was tall and strong of thigh. She wore red lipstick and violet eye shadow. When she stood she was finely postured. Her hair was big and it touched the head-liner of the car. Jones thought of her as a stallion, if a stallion could be female. Surely they had a name for girl horses, but he couldn't recall it. Aside from prison time, and a West Virginia childhood he barely recalled, he had rarely been outside the city.

"He's in there," said Jones, looking up to the face of the red-brick apartment house on the northeast corner of R. In a second-floor window, against a frayed curtain, was the sil-houette of a small man.

"How you know it's him?"

"That's his itty-bitty shadow."

"Could be a kid."

"He tiny like one. But it's him."

"Maybe he got a girl up there."

"Last time Bobby Odum had a girl, a black man was in the White House."

"Wasn't never no black president."

"And he ain't had no pussy *since* then."

Coco's shoulders shook as she issued a low laugh. Smoke dribbled through her painted lips.

"Leave it run," said Jones.

He got out of the Plymouth and crossed the street in long strides. He, too, was tall. He wore patch-pocket jeans and two-tone brown Flagg Brothers stacks with three-inch heels and curlicue white stitching on the vamps. His loud-print rayon shirt, tails-out, had collars big as spears. His nose had been broken and left unset. He had very light skin, and his face and hard body were prominently freckled and moled.

His ratty blowout was the color of rust and its unpicked, misshapen form gave him a general air of I-don't-give-a-fuck. He was as he appeared to be.

Jones entered the building at 13th and R through a glass door set between nonfunctioning gas lanterns. He walked up a flight of stairs and stopped on the second-floor landing, which smelled of cigarettes and marijuana. In the air was the thump of bass coming from the stereo of one of the residents below, and he could feel it pulse through the wood floor. He came to the scarred door that he knew opened to the apartment of Bobby Odum, knocked on the door roughly, after a while heard a muddled voice say, "Who it is?" and he answered, "Red."

The door opened. Odum, wearing plaid pants and a silk shirt open to expose a ladder of chest bones, stood a few steps back from the frame. The black stacks on his feet elevated him but somehow managed to make him look smaller. He was the size of Sammy Davis Jr. but lacked his talent. Plus, Sammy got all that play, and Odum got none. Even the whores, retailing their licorice on what was left of the 14th Street stroll, chuckled when he pulled out his money, cracking on him while they palmed his bread. Bring your twin brother, you got one, and strap him 'cross your ass so you don't fall in. Ha ha ha. Almost made Jones sorry for Odum. Almost.

Odum forced a smile. "Red."

"It is me."

"What brings you here, brother?"

"My money does." Jones entered the apartment and closed the door behind him.

Odum stood before him, flexing and unflexing his hands. Sweat had appeared on his dark, deeply lined forehead. His eyes told Jones that he was high.

"You want a drink, somethin?"

"I could."

"Let me treat you to some Regal."

"Pour it," said Jones.

Odum went to a rolling cart displaying liquor and setups, and free-poured scotch into a clouded tumbler from a Chivas bottle. The bottle had been filled and refilled over the years with off-brands, its label faded to gray. It now held Scots Lion, the low-shelf brand from the Continental liquor shop on Vermont Avenue.

Odum handed Jones his drink, and Jones hit it. It tasted like scotch. He pointed to the sofa and said, "Sit down."

Odum had a seat on the sofa and Jones settled into an overstuffed chair. Between them, a coffee table was littered with burned bottle caps, cotton balls pink with blood, a two-dollar necktie, and a large metal ashtray.

Jones reached into his breast pocket and pulled out a pack of Kools that was unopened on top. He shook a smoke from the hole he had torn out of the bottom of the pack, flipped the cigarette, and put the filtered end in his mouth. He picked a book of fire up off the table, read its face, and struck a match, touching flame to tobacco and taking in a deep lungful of menthol. He let the smoke out slow.

"So you been past Ed Murphy's," said Jones, his eyes going to the matchbook before he helped himself and slipped it into his pocket.

"I caught that boy Hathaway at the Supper Club. He was playin there last week. Donny's a Howard man."

"My woman's into him. And that female he be singin with, too."

"They gonna be together at the Carter Barron," said Odum. "I got tickets for the show." His face soured as he realized his mistake.

"Where the tickets at?" said Jones.

"They in my leather," muttered Odum, angry at himself. Something else came to him, and his tone betrayed him as he pointedly added, "The *in*side pocket."

Jones dragged on his Kool, double-dragged, leaned forward, and tapped ash into the tray. He stared at Odum and said nothing.

"Red?"

"Uh-huh?"

"*Shit*, Red, I been lookin to get up with you."

"You have?"

"You ain't give me no number, though."

"I called *you* and got nary an answer."

"That's funny, 'cause I been here."

"Maybe your phone line's fucked up. We could check it right now and find out."

"Nah. You must got the number wrong, somethin."

"Decatur two, four seven nine five?"

"That's it."

"Then I ain't get nothin wrong. *Did* I?"

"Okay."

"Where my money at?" said Jones.

Odum spread his hands. "Wasn't but eighty dollars, Red."

"One or eighty, it's all the same to me. You played and you lost. Trying to be funny with a ten and no royalty. Now you need to make it right."

What Jones said was true. There was a card game and Odum had stayed in on a ten-high, looking to outlast Jones and the others on a bluff. Jones, who did not fold, had been holding a pair of faces. But a weak hand and eighty dollars was not why Jones had come.

"You can have my watch," said Odum.

"I don't want that off-brand shit."

"I got heroin."

"How much?"

Odum tapped the toe of his right Jarman on the wood floor. "One dime is all."

"What am I supposed to do with that?"

"I don't know. Look, I'm just a tester, man—"

"Where you get your medicine at?"

"Ah, shit, Red."

"Where?"

Odum lowered his eyes. "Dude named Roland Williams. He got bundles."

"Roland Williams, went to Cardozo?"

"Nah, not *Ro-Ro* Williams. I'm talking about Long Nose Roland, came out of Roosevelt. He been going up top. You know, coppin at that spot in Harlem they call Little Baltimore."

"Where Long Nose stay at?"

"Thirteen hundred block of T," said Odum.

"Where exactly?"

Odum did not know the address. He described the row house by the color of its shutters and the little porch out front. Jones saw it in his head.

"Okay," said Jones. He drank from the tumbler, emptied it, and placed it roughly on the coffee table. He dropped his cigarette into the glass and rose from the couch as if sprung.

"We done?" said Odum.

"Put some music on the box," said Jones. "It's too quiet in this hole."

Odum got up. His feet were unsteady beneath him as he crossed the room. He went to the home entertainment center he had purchased, on time, for one hundred and forty-eight dollars at the Sun Radio uptown. He had not paid on it for many months. It was an eighty-watt Webcor system with a record changer and dust cover housed atop an AM/FM stereo receiver and eight-track player. Two air-suspension speakers bookended the unit, seated on a slotted metal stand holding Odum's vinyl.

Odum chose an album and slipped it out of its dust jacket. He placed the record on the turntable, side two up, and carefully dropped the tone arm on the first song. Psychedelic funk came forward.

Odum did not turn around. As the groove hit him, he began to move with a small, off-the-rhythm dip and a shake of his hips. He was not much of a dancer. He forced himself to smile.

"*Free Your Mind and Your Ass Will Follow*," said Odum.

Jones, now standing behind the couch, said nothing.

" 'I wanna know if it's good to you,' " sang Odum, as the chorus kicked in. His mouth had gone dry and he licked his lips. "Wait till you hear Eddie Hazel's *gui*tar on the way out the jam. Eddie can do it."

"Turn it up," said Jones. Odum hiked up the volume. "More," said Jones. Odum's trembling hand clockwised the dial. "Now sit your narrow ass back down." The music was loud in the room. It had been mixed to travel from speaker to speaker, and its freaks-in-the-funhouse effect made Jones cold. Odum sat on the couch, his birdlike hands folded in his lap.

"Red," said Odum.

"Hush," said Jones.

"Red, please, man . . . I'll get you your eighty."

"This ain't about no eighty. It's about you runnin your gums."

"*Please.*"

"You a churchgoin man?"

"I try to be."

"All that bullshit the preacher been tellin you? About that better world you gonna find on the other side?"

"*Red.*"

"You about to see if it's true."

Jones drew a .22 Colt from beneath the tails of his rayon, put the barrel behind Odum's ear, and squeezed the trigger. Odum said, "Huh," and as he lurched forward, blood flowed from his mouth and splashed onto the coffee table, and Jones put another round into the back of his head. Odum voided his bowels, and the smell of his evacuation and the one-cent smell of blood were fast in the room.

Jones reholstered the .22 in the dip of his bells. He found the concert tickets in Odum's leather and slipped them into one of his patch pockets. Then he recalled Bobby Odum directing him, almost desperately, to a particular place in the jacket, and his suspicious nature told him to search the jacket further.

He put his hand into the left side pocket of the leather and retrieved a woman's ring the color of gold. Its mount carried a large center stone, clear and bright, surrounded by eight smaller stones orbiting around it. To the untrained eye it could have been a cluster of diamonds, but Jones was certain that he was looking at rhinestones or plain old glass. Long as Jones had known him, Odum had been ass broke.

It was a fake piece, for sure. But it was pretty, and Coco would like the way it looked on her hand. Jones slipped the ring into his patch pocket, too.

He took the glass he had been drinking from and carried it with him, wiping the doorknob off with his sleeve as he exited, listening to the guitarist going off from the stereo. The little man had been right. That cat Hazel could play.

Out on 13th, Jones crossed the street. A man named Milton Wallace sat on the concrete edging of a row house lawn, smoking down a cigarette he had resurrected from a nearby gutter. Wallace watched Jones pass.

Jones got into the Fury's passenger bucket. He handed the tickets to Coco and said, "These for you, baby."

Coco's eyes came alive as she studied one of the tickets. "Donny and Roberta at the Carter Barron? *Thank* you, Red."

"Ain't no thing."

"Bobby give these to you?"

"He can't use 'em no more." Jones placed the scotch glass on the mat between his feet. "I got somethin else for you, too."

"Show me, baby."

"When we get to your crib. We need to leave outta here now." Jones pointed to the keys hanging in the ignition. "Cook it, Coco."

She turned the key, engaged the transmission, and pulled away from the curb.

Milton Wallace eyed the Fury as it traveled south on 13th. Wallace recorded the image of the car, and the license plate, in his head.

TWO

SHE WAS stepping out of a Warwick-blue Firebird convertible, sitting on redline tires, when Strange first saw her. She had parked the Pontiac on 9th, near the Upshur Street cross. She was young, had prominent cheekbones and clean beige skin, wore her hair in a big natural, and was unrestrained in a print halter dress. The girl was fine. Purse in hand, her hips moving with a feline sway.

Looked to Strange that she was headed toward his spot. He could see her clearly through the wide plate glass window fronting his business. One of the reasons he liked this place: the open view.

He got up out of the swivel chair behind his metal desk. A hard desk-style chair, like the kind he'd had in high school, sat before it. He looked around with an eye to straightening up, but there wasn't much to put in place. He had one of those new machines, recorded the phone calls when they came in, but he had not yet figured out how to use it. He'd been here for just four months or so, and he had only acquired the bare bones that a person needed to replicate the look of an office. Everything seemed temporary. Even the sign out front was a bullshit sign, done by a dude around the corner who called himself an artist but claimed he was a lot of things when he was high.

A radial GE clock radio sat on his desk, plugged into a floor socket. Its AM dial was set on WOL. The sound was all treble, no bass. Amid the static, "Family Affair" was playing low, Sly and his drugged-out drawl.

A little bell mounted over the door chimed as the woman entered the shop. Strange, tall and broad shouldered, wearing low-rise bells, a wide black belt, brass-eye stacks, a rayon shirt stretched out across his chest, and a thick Roundtree mustache, stepped up to greet her.

"Are you Mr. Strange?"

"I am. But call me Derek, or Strange. Either way's fine with me. No need to call me mister."

"My name is Maybelline Walker."

"Pleasure."

"Can I take some of your time? I'll be brief."

Strange shook her hand and took in her smell, the faint sweetness of strawberries. "Let's sit."

They crossed the cool linoleum floor. Strange allowed her to go ahead so he could check out her behind, as a man will tend to do. He made a maître d's hand motion, pointing her to the client chair. She fitted herself into it, glanced at its attached desktop with puzzlement, and rested her forearm atop its face as she crossed one bare leg over the other. Strange noticed the ripple of muscle in her thigh as he took a seat behind his desk.

"What can I do for you today?"

"I've been seeing your sign out front for months now."

"I'm fixin to get a new one."

"Strange Investigations. Do you have many?"

"A few."

Background checks, mainly, thought Strange. Case-builds for divorce lawyers. Infidelity tails. Nothing of any weight.

"Are you busy with one now?"

"I'm in a slow period."

"Hmm."

Strange looked her over. Straight backed and poised. Had some nice titties on her, too. High and tight, big old erasers about to bust through the fabric of her dress. A redbone with light-brown eyes. One of those brown-paper-bag gals, the kind he'd rarely gone after, as dark-skinned women were more to his liking. Not that he wouldn't straighten out Miss Maybelline Walker if she'd give him a go-sign. God, he would hit the hell out of it if he had the chance.

"Is there something?"

"What?" said Strange.

"You're looking at me...well." Maybelline blushed, a little.

"I'm just waitin on you to tell me what this is about, Miss Walker."

"Make it Maybelline."

"Go ahead."

Maybelline took a deep, theatrical breath. "I lost a piece of jewelry. A ring. I'd like you to find it and bring it back to me. I'll pay you for your time, of course, and a bonus if you succeed."

"How do you mean *lost*, exactly?"

"I loaned the ring to an acquaintance of mine. He said that he had an associate who could appraise it. You know, to see if it had any real value."

Strange knew the meaning of the word *appraise*, but he did not make an issue of her condescension. If she was one of these uppity, educated girls, if she thought she was better than him because of geography, high school, skin color, or whatever, it made no difference to him. A job was sitting across the desk from him, and that meant cash money, something for which he had need.

"And your acquaintance, he, what, took off with the ring?"

"He was murdered."

Strange sat forward in his chair. He picked up a pencil that he had been using to draw the design of a logo he intended to implement on a new sign for out front, in the event that he ever had enough money to purchase one. He'd put the logo on his cards, too, when he got around to having some printed. He'd been playing with a magnifying glass laid partially over the name of his business, but as of yet he had not gotten it exactly right.

"So now the ring's missing," said Strange.

"Yes."

Strange opened a schoolboy notebook and looked at Maybelline.

"The name of your acquaintance?"

"Robert Odum. Went by Bobby."

"When was this? His murder, I mean."

"A week ago yesterday. He was shot to death in his residence."

"Gimme the address."

Maybelline told him where Odum stayed and Strange wrote it down. He vaguely remembered reading about the murder in the *Post*, buried in the section locals called "Violent Negro Deaths."

"Why was Odum killed?" said Strange. "Any idea?"

"I don't know why anyone would want to hurt Bobby. He was gentle."

"You knew him long?"

"Not very. He was a friend of a friend." She held her eyes on his. "I like to think I'm a good judge of character."

"How you know the ring's gone?"

"I've been by his apartment since his death. I looked everywhere for it."

"Police let you in?"

"No. I spoke to a detective, but he told me I couldn't pass through. I waited until they were done working the . . . what do you call that?"

"The crime scene."

"It was several days after Bobby's death that I went by."

"How'd you get into his place?"

"I have a key."

"But you say you were only an acquaintance."

"We'd grown close in a short period of time. Bobby trusted me."

"If he was going to a fence with your ring—"

"I didn't say he was going to a fence."

"Okay. Where'd you get the ring, originally?"

"I'm not sure I like your tone."

"No offense intended," said Strange.

Maybelline's eyes flickered delicately with forgiveness. "The ring was in my family. It was my mother's. *Her* mother's before that. It's costume jewelry, you want the truth. But it means something to me."

"I understand. Still, if it was only costume jewelry, why was Odum getting it appraised for you?"

"He seemed to think that the body of it, the ring itself, I mean, was gold. Obviously the stones were cheap glass, but gold, of course, has value. I didn't care about its worth. I wasn't ever going to sell it. But for insurance purposes, I thought it was a good idea."

"All right." Strange was tiring of her story, which was illogical and probably a lie. It had begun to confuse him, and maybe that was her intent. Still, he was curious. "Describe the ring, please."

"But I haven't decided to hire you yet," she said, rather petulantly.

"I can provide references if you want."

"That won't be necessary. Tell me something about your background."

"I'm D.C. born and bred. Grew up in Park View, on Princeton. Went to high school at Roosevelt, right across the street from where we sit. I was Four-F 'cause of a knee injury I got while playing football for the Rough Riders. My knee is good now, and as you can see I'm perfectly fit. I was an officer with the MPD until the riots, at which time I left the force. Kicked around some, doing a little bit of this and that, until I figured out that I dug detective work but not a uniform. So I copped a license and opened up my own place. I like soul and funk, the Redskins, good-looking women,

Western movies, half-smokes, nice cars, puppy dogs, and long walks on the beach. Hot oils, too, if the situation calls for it."

This time Maybelline blushed full. She smiled and said, "I guess that almost covers it."

"Almost?"

"Why have a storefront here when you could operate out of your car? What I mean is, what does paying rent get you when your business is done mostly on the street?"

"It's an odd question."

"I'd like to know if my money is going to your overhead or to shoe leather."

"Fair enough. Kids in this neighborhood watch me open that front door every morning. I think it's important for them to see a young black man going to work each day, building his own thing. Don't you?"

"Yes."

"So there it is. Now tell me something about you."

"If you're looking to know more about me, here's not the time or place."

"Okay, then," said Strange. "The ring?"

"It has a large center stone, looks like a diamond, with eight smaller stones circling around it. The arrangement is called a cluster. The ring it's mounted on has the Grecian key design engraved on its shoulders on a background of black enamel."

As she spoke, Strange drew a version of the ring, based on her description. When he was done he turned the notebook around and let her look at it.

"Close?"

"Something like that," she said. "What do you charge?"

"I get eight dollars an hour. My hours are straight and I'll account for all of them. I ask for a fifty-dollar retainer at the start."

"I can give that to you right now if you'd like."

"That would be good."

She reached into the small rectangular purse and counted out some bills. She handed Strange his fee across the desk.

"What do you do, Maybelline, you don't mind my askin?"

"I'm a tutor," she said. "Mathematics."

"Which school?"

"In-home. I work by the hour, just like you."

"Let me get your contact information right quick."

She took the notebook and pencil, and wrote down her phone number and home address. As she did it, "Mr. Big Stuff" came from the clock radio on the desk. Strange saw her nod her head to the rhythm and the syncopated shake of one of her feet.

"You like this one?"

"Hard to get it out of my head. OL doesn't help, either. They play it all the time."

"All groove, no melody," said Strange. "But what a groove."

Jean Knight, he thought, from New Orleans. Stax single number double-0-88. Originally recorded for the Malaco/Chimneyville label out of Jackson, Mississippi. Strange still catalogued this arcane data in his mind.

"The singer is a southern girl, right?"

"Uh-huh. But this radio does her no justice. I need to get a real stereo in here."

"All in time."

Maybelline got up out of her seat. Strange did the same.

"Have you reported the missing ring to the police?"

"*Please.* I'm not even trying to waste my time."

Strange nodded. "I'll be in touch. Thanks for your confidence."

"That ring is dear to me. My mother passed last year and it's what I have left of her."

"I'll do my best to find it." As he walked her to the front door, he said, "Do you know if the MPD has a lead on Odum's killer?"

"The homicide policeman I spoke with barely told me anything."

"You recall his name?"

"Frank Vaughn," said Maybelline. "White man, on the old side. Do you know of him?"

"Heard tell of him, yes."

In fact, Strange knew Vaughn well.

THREE

HE WORE his hair a little bit longer now, just over his ears. What they called the dry look. No more flattop, no more Brylcreem. Even Sinatra's hair was on the long side, though that Hail Caesar thing he'd tried for a while was all wrong for his face and age. That was around the time he'd married that skinny young actress. Vaughn reckoned that Sinatra was just scared. Scared of death, like all sane men and, worse, scared of being irrelevant. At least Frank Vaughn had not made those kinds of mistakes. An updated hairstyle, sure. But no leisure suits, no Roman Empire cuts, no May–December romances. Vaughn knew who he was.

He studied himself in the mirror as he straightened his black tie and smoothed out the lapels of his gray Robert Hall suit. A bit more jowly in the face, some baggage under the eyes, but not too gone for fifty-two years old.

Vaughn smiled, displaying his widely spaced, crooked teeth. The younger cops called him "Hound Dog," on account of his look. He'd heard one of the uniforms say,

"Vaughn looks like a animated canine," trying to be fancy with it, when all he meant was, he looked like that big dog in the cartoons, the one with the scary choppers and the spiked collar. Vaughn preferred to think of himself as a less pretty Mitchum. Or Sinatra on the cover of that record *No One Cares*, seated at the bar in raincoat and fedora, staring into his shot glass. A night wolf, wounded and alone.

"What're you grinning at?" said Olga, who had entered their bedroom, her hands on her pedal-pushered hips, watching him appraising himself in the full-length. Olga's hair, as black and dead as a stuffed raven, had been newly coiffed at the Vincent et Vincent in Wheaton Plaza. *Et*. Vaughn always wondered why they didn't just say "and" on the sign.

"Just admiring my good looks," said Vaughn.

"Lord, you're vain," said Olga, smiling crookedly, her bright-red lipstick screaming out against her mime-white face.

"When you got it," said Vaughn.

"Got what?"

"This." Vaughn turned, brought her into his arms, and pushed his manhood against her, to let her know he was still there. They kissed dryly.

"What have you got today?" she said, as he broke away and walked over to the nightstand by his side of the bed.

"Police work, Olga," he said, his usual reply. He withdrew his holstered service revolver, a .38 Special, from the nightstand drawer, checked the load, and clipped the rig onto his belt line. "Ricky home?"

Ricky, their college graduate, pacing himself as a bartender at a little live music venue in Bethesda. Vaughn had always feared Ricky would be a swish, with his long hair and mania for music, but the kid got more pussy than a hetero hairdresser. These days he was shacked up with a broad somewhere more often than he was in their house.

"He didn't make it back last night," said Olga. "But he called so we wouldn't worry."

"Loverboy," said Vaughn, with sarcasm and pride.

"Stop."

He kissed her again, this time on her cheek, wondering idly what she was going to do all day. He left their master bedroom and headed down the stairs, noticing a line of dirt along the baseboards of the living room as he grabbed his raincoat out of the foyer closet. Olga tried, but she wasn't much for housekeeping. Their place hadn't been spick-and-span since they'd lost their maid, Alethea Strange, just after the '68 riots. He'd driven her to her row home in Park View, right through the thick of it as the city burned, and though it was unsaid, he knew she would never return to their house as a domestic. It had been so. Vaughn bringing her up in his mind, feeling a stir, thinking, That was some kind of woman.

He left their house, a split level off Georgia Avenue between downtown Silver Spring and Wheaton, and drove toward D.C., his mood brightening considerably as he rolled over the District line, nearing the action, the final passion that moved his blood.

VAUGHN HAD recently bought a new Monaco from the Dodge dealership in Laurel, Maryland. The Monaco was a middle-aged man's car, gold with a brown vinyl roof, a four-door with power steering, power windows, and power brakes, but heavy, with too little power under the hood. He missed his white-over-red '67 Polara with the 318 and cat-eye taillights, and he missed the decade it came from. Those had been violent years, volatile, sexy, fun.

Vaughn drove down 16th Street, came to a stop at a red light, nodded to a couple of patrolmen in a squad car idling alongside him. That was something he wouldn't have seen five years ago, two blacks in uniform, riding together in the same car.

The MPD had integrated fully now, the ratio of black cops to white more accurately reflecting the population makeup of the city, which, post-riot white flight, had settled to near 80 percent colored. Vaughn had to watch that, you couldn't call them colored anymore, or Negro for that matter. Olga told him time and time again, "They're African American, you big ox." Vaughn had no major problem with the designation, but he figured, if they're going to call me white, and sometimes whitey, I'm just gonna go ahead and call them black. That is, if I can remember.

Okay, Olga?

Vaughn parked in a lot beside the Third District headquarters at 16th and V. No more precincts, but districts now. He checked in, sat at his desk and made a couple of calls, left the building, and headed back to his Monaco. Under its dash he had installed a two-way radio. He rarely kept it turned on.

A young uniform saw Vaughn in the lot and said, "How's it hangin, Hound Dog?"

Vaughn said, "Long and strong."

He lit an L&M and pulled out of the lot.

*   *   *

VAUGHN PARKED the Dodge on 13th Street, near the corner of R, and entered the apartment building with the extinguished gas lanterns where Bobby Odum had resided and been chilled. There was music bleeding out into the hallway, but it was not coming from the unit he was headed for. He went there straightaway and with his fist he cop-knocked on the front door.

The door opened shortly thereafter. A young black woman with a big Afro stood in the frame. She had on high-waisted slacks and a macramé vest over a sky-blue shirt. She was compact, but her rope wedge shoes gave her altitude. Her eyes were deep set and intelligent, and he imagined that they could be welcoming if directed at the right individual. Directed at Vaughn, they were ice cool.

"Janet Newman?"

"Jan*ette*."

"I'm Detective Vaughn," he said, flipping open his badge case and replacing it quickly in the flap pocket of his jacket. "Thanks for seeing me."

"I don't have much time."

"I won't take much. May I come in?"

She stepped aside and allowed him to pass through. The place was neat and clean, with brown carpeting and what Vaughn thought of as African decor on the walls. Masks, wood carvings, shit like that. Least there weren't any spears. The Mother Country stuff was the rage with these young ones.

A stick of incense burned in a ceramic holder formed as a miniature elephant, set on a living-room table near a sofa-and-chair arrangement. The room's sole window had its curtain drawn.

Janette Newman did not close the door. She stood beside it and folded her arms across her chest. Vaughn guessed that he would not be offered a beverage, nor would he be asked to have a seat. It was hard to think straight or have a conversation, what with the music bleeding into the hall. He knew where it was coming from. He had interviewed the unit's occupants, a mother with a job and her son, a doper who had no plan to get one. Kid listened to music all day long. What Ricky would call soul-funk. It was all Zulu-jump to Vaughn.

"You're a hard woman to pin down," said Vaughn.

"I work," said Janette.

"You teach over at Tubman, right?"

"Correct. There was a flood, so they closed the school today."

"Kind of young to have a teaching position, aren't you?" He thought his words complimentary until he saw her eyes harden.

"I have a degree from Howard. Would you like to see my diploma?"

"No disrespect intended," said Vaughn. "I meant, you know, you're doing well for such a young woman."

Janette looked him over. "You had some questions?"

"You stated over the phone that you weren't here at the time of Robert Odum's murder."

"I was in my classroom when it happened."

"Did you know him?"

"Not to speak to, past a nod or a 'good morning.' "

"He had people visit him from time to time, didn't he?"

"Most folks do."

"Was there one by the name of Maybelline Walker? Light-skinned woman, young, attractive..."

"If I saw visitors I don't remember them."

"Not a one."

"I said no."

"Do you recall if Odum had a job?"

"I wouldn't know."

Vaughn already had Odum's work address, as he'd found a pay stub in his apartment. He was testing her. She was withholding information, and probably lying, but not because she had anything to do with Odum's death. Some folks just didn't care for white people or police.

"You sure about that?" said Vaughn.

He gazed at her for a long moment until she became uncomfortable and looked away. He liked her backbone, and he didn't even mind her attitude, but she wasn't in his physical wheelhouse. If he was going to go black, he'd go for a specific look: cream in the coffee, white features. A Lena Horne type.

"You're staring at me," she said.

"I was thinking."

"Of what?"

"My case."

"Don't you have any leads?"

"I can't speak on that at this time."

"Be nice if the police told us something so we could rest easy in this building. I'm not tryin to get myself killed around here."

Vaughn reached into his inside pocket. "Here's my card. Anything comes to mind, give me a call."

Vaughn walked out of her apartment without another word and heard the door close behind him. Janette was not a person of interest. Just another name he could cross off the list.

He went through the hall, the bass still coming from the adjoining unit, the glass door of the building buzzing from it as he pushed on its surface, exiting to breathe fresh air.

Outside, a man, an addict or alcoholic from the used-up look of his eyes, sat on a nearby retaining wall, smoking a cigarette. Vaughn approached and showed him his badge. The man did not seem impressed. Vaughn offered him ten dollars, and the offer was waved away. Then he offered to buy him a bottle in exchange for his time. The man declined. Vaughn asked him a couple of questions, got nothing but shrugs.

Two strikes, thought Vaughn. And: I am hungry.

HE HAD lunch at the counter of the Hot Shoppes on Georgia Avenue, in Brightwood Park, up around Hamilton. In its parking lot had been the famous fight between three badass white greasers and a dozen or so motivated coloreds, back in the '60s. The fight had carried over to the other side of the street. Those white boys could mix it up. That kind of balls-out, bare-knuckled hate conflict was done now, too, thought Vaughn with nostalgia. The blacks had taken over the city, and race rumbles had gone the way of drop-down Chevys, Link Wray club dates, and Ban-Lon shirts.

Vaughn had a Mighty Mo burger, onion rings, and an orange freeze, then followed it up with a hunk of hot fudge cake and a cup of coffee. The perfect local lunch. Pulling the coffee cup and an ashtray in front of him, he used his customized Zippo lighter, a map of Okinawa inlaid on its face, to light an L&M.

Bobby Odum. A pathetic character, one hundred and twenty-three pounds of junkie, a former second-story man now scraping by as a dishwasher and heroin tester. He was one of many confidential informants that Vaughn kept and cultivated around the city. Testers and cut buddies made the best, most vulnerable CIs because they were addicts. They always had need of money.

The ballistics report had determined that the slugs retrieved from Odum's apartment came from a .22, a weapon favored by assassins who worked close in. A Colt Woodsman, if Vaughn was to make a wager.

Odum had recently given Vaughn information related to a homicide, a tip on a man involved in a Northeast burn. The resulting warrant had led to a home search, the discovery of the murder weapon, and the arrest of one James Carpenter, now in the D.C. Jail awaiting trial.

The last time Vaughn and Odum had met was at a diner called Frank's Carry Out, on the 1700 block of 14th Street. The owner, Pete Frank, had allowed Vaughn to talk to Odum privately, in the storage room at the rear of the building. That day, Odum had been worried running to paranoid. He claimed it had gotten around that he and Vaughn, well-known by the District's underworld, had been seen together in Shaw, and that it had then been assumed that he, Odum, had fingered Carpenter. He told Vaughn that his apartment phone had been ringing "off the hook," and that it was, he suspected, some "wrong dude" who was looking to find him.

Vaughn asked him if he knew the caller's name, but Odum claimed he had no clue.

"How you know it's not a woman calling you," said Vaughn, "or a friend?"

"I know," said Odum, touching a finger to his chest. "I feel that shit, right in here. The reaper 'bout to *come* at me, Frank."

Vaughn slipped him twenty dollars. "Go get well," he said.

The next time Vaughn saw Odum, he was lying on a slab in the city morgue, the top of his head sawed off, one eye blown out of his gray face.

Vaughn tapped ash and wondered if it was him that got Odum killed. Not that they were friends, but he felt a sense of responsibility, if not accountability, to see to it that Odum's killer was found. Bobby was just a little guy he paid for information. But it didn't matter to Vaughn who Odum was, or what color he was, or if they were asshole buddies or not. Vaughn worked all of his cases the same way.

He dragged on his cigarette and signaled the counter girl for his check.

VAUGHN DROVE down to 14th and U, once the epicenter of black Washington, now a weak reminder of its former vibrant life since its burning in '68.

He was in search of Martina Lewis. Whores were out on the street at night, witnessed all kinds of illicit events, gossiped out of boredom, and, because they were young, had good retention. Also, they were easily shook down. But Vaughn had never put his foot to Martina's neck. He'd not had to.

As it was afternoon, the prostitutes had woken up, were eating breakfast and getting prepared for work, but they were not yet visible on the stroll. In a popular diner on U, Vaughn got up with a stocky streetwalker, went by Gina Marie, who claimed she'd heard nothing about the Odum murder. Though she had given him no information, he put a five in her callused hand.

Vaughn paid for a ticket at the nearby Lincoln Theatre box office. After allowing his eyes to adjust to the darkness, he found Martina Lewis seated in one of the middle rows of the near-empty auditorium. Martina was napping, head back, wig askew, lipsticked mouth slightly open, with an Adam's apple as big as a fist. It was said that Martina was hung like a donkey, too. Some men were fooled, and some claimed to be, but most knew what he was and wanted it. Martina had been in the life, and successful at it, for some time.

Buck and the Preacher was onscreen, Poitier and Belafonte in Western drag. Vaughn watched it and was quickly bored. He felt that the movie was like the other ones, popular these days, where all the black guys were heroes and studs and the whites were racists, trashmen, or queers. Vaughn shook Martina's shoulder until he awakened.

Martina was startled at first but then settled into a brief and very quiet conversation with the detective he knew as Frank and who many on the street called Hound Dog. Frank had always showed Martina something close to respect. Frank had never threatened Martina or pressured him for sex. Most important, Frank paid the rate, including the extra for the room.

When Vaughn had what he'd come for, he gave Martina thirty-five dollars and left the auditorium. Now he had something concrete.

"The dude you're looking for," Martina had said, "goes by Red."

"That's it?" said Vaughn. "Just Red?"

"I heard him called Red Fury, too. I don't know why."

"No Christian name. No last name, either."

"Red's all I know," said Martina, telling Vaughn a prudent lie. Wasn't any kind of accident that Martina Lewis was a survivor.

Out on U Street, Vaughn lit a cigarette. Red was a fairly common street name for light-skinned, light-haired black dudes, but thinking hard on it, no specific Reds came to mind. Still, it was a start.

Vaughn would go to the station and search through the cards, where the rap sheet descriptions included known a.k.a.'s. But not just yet. He was energized.

LINDA ALLEN lived in an apartment in the Woodnor, on 16th, near the bridge end-capped with the statues of lions. She was a secretary at the Arnold and Porter law firm on the 1200 block of 19th, and Vaughn had been calling on her here for almost fifteen years. Linda was his special friend.

She greeted him at the door in a spring-blue dress that showed off her upper curves and a pair of Andrew Geller heels that did justice to her calves. A leggy brunette on the downward slope of her forties, she was tall and healthy, with pleasingly muscled thighs and the big firm rack of a straight-off-the-farm centerfold. Linda had never married or given birth, which no doubt explained her still-youthful figure. Twenty-year-old studs did double takes when she walked down the street.

"How's it goin, doll?" said Vaughn.

"Better now," said Linda, and she nudged the door closed with her foot and came into his arms. They kissed passionately and Vaughn felt his pants get tight.

"Glad to see me?" His sharp white teeth gleamed in the lamplight of the living room.

"I need a shower, handsome. Fix us some drinks."

"Keep your shoes on," said Vaughn.

Vaughn put a Chris Connor record on Linda's console stereo, built a couple of Beam rocks from her bar cart, and took the cocktails into her bedroom. The water was running behind her bathroom door.

He took off his jacket, tie, pants, socks, and shoes, and sat on the edge of the bed, feeling himself unwind with each sip of bourbon. A little while later, Linda came naked and scented into the room, the high-heeled Gellers refitted on her feet. She picked up her drink off the nightstand, took a long pull of it, and stood there proudly, in profile, letting him look at her because she knew he liked to. Soon he had her split atop the sheets, the missionary man, in control, giving it to her without the word *lovemaking* entering either of their minds, his thick, helmeted cock plunging in and out of her warm, wet box, a pure physical act, which was what both of them were there for. Afterward, smoking cigarettes and finishing their drinks with the sex smell lingering in the room, laughing easily, talking softly, never about anything serious or with the pretense of plans, because Vaughn loved his wife, and Linda understood that this was something else.

Linda's fingers traced the fading shoulder tattoo Vaughn had gotten one drunken night in the Pacific, twenty-seven years ago. "Olga," written across a flowing banner, scripted on a deep-red heart.

"What're you working on these days, Frank?"

Vaughn said, "A case."

FOUR

COCO WATKINS'S place of business was located on 14th, Northwest, between R and S, on the second floor of an old row house. On the ground floor was a neighborhood market, once a DGS store owned and operated by a Jew, now run by an ambitious Puerto Rican. Fourteenth, from U Street north to Park Road, had gone up in flames the night of Dr. King's assassination, and though the major fires had not burned this far south, the event had made the once-grand street a near commercial dead zone. But not every enterprise had been negatively affected. There was still a steady nightly stream of customers, married suburbanites and white teenage boys looking to lose their virginity, who kept one part of the local economy alive.

Coco was a madam, technically, but the title meant nothing more than manager for a multi-bed operation housing six small, cut-up rooms, each of which held a bare mattress, a particleboard dresser, a freestanding rack with wire hangers, and a low-watt lamp. The girls made their connections out on the street, leaning into the open windows of idling cars, and handed over the prepaid fee, thirty for the act, five for the room, to Coco before entering with their johns.

There was no pimp involved in this particular operation. It was fairly unusual for a woman to have such unchallenged control over a stable, but it was known that Robert Lee Jones was Coco's man, and Red's hard rep was such that she stayed protected. Even when Jones was incarcerated, few had tried to mack on Coco's women.

Coco and Jones sat in her office, which fronted 14th. A nice big room with a bar, a king-size, brass-headboard bed, red velvet couch and chairs, desk, compact stereo, and a couple of windows giving to a view of the wide street below. Coco was lounging on the couch in a negligee, her hair high and elegant, a live Viceroy in hand, the cluster-stone ring on her finger. Jones was in a chair, using an oiled cloth to polish one of two .45s he owned, classic Colts with stainless slides and black checkered grips. He had broken the .22 on a guardrail near the Anacostia and thrown its pieces into the river.

"Where you about to go with that heater?" said Coco.

"Me and Fonzo got business."

"Contract?"

"Freelance."

"Be mindful. The Odum thing's still warm."

"They got nothin."

"What I been hearin, that Detective Vaughn caught the case."

"The one they call Hound Dog."

"Him. Girl I know name Gina Marie told me he been askin around."

"Least they put a man on it."

Coco dragged on her cigarette. "That dude got no quit."

"Do I look like I care?"

After coming to the city from West Virginia at an early age, Jones had grown up in one of D.C.'s infamous alley dwellings, way below the poverty line. No father in his life, ever, with hustlers in and out the spot, taking the place of one. A mother who worked domestic when she could. Half brothers and sisters he barely knew or kept track of. Twenty-five dollars a month rent, and his mother could rarely come up with it. All of them hungry, all the time. Being poor in that extreme way, Jones felt that nothing after could cut too deep. Take what you want, take no man's shit. No police can intimidate you, no sentence will enslave you, no cell can contain your mind.

Jones stood, holstered the .45 in the dip of his bells, dropped the tail of his shirt over the bulge. His chest looked flat under clothing, but he was just shy of concrete. Five hundred push-ups a day in lockup, the same regimen on the outside. Legend was, an ambitious young dude had tried to shank him in jail and the blade had broken off in Red's chest. It wasn't a legend. Homemade shiv, but still.

"My Fury's in the alley," said Coco.

"We taking Fonzo's short," said Jones. He bent down, kissed her full red mouth. His fingers grazed the inside of her bare thigh, and she got damp.

"Will I see you tonight?"

"Bet," said Jones.

He left the room and walked down the hall, where a young working woman, a big mark above her lip, stood outside a room in a sheer slip, huffing a smoke.

"Red," she said.

"Girl."

Out on 14th, Alfonzo Jefferson pulled up in his '68 Electra, a gold-over-black convertible with 360 horses, a Turbo-400 trans, wide whitewalls, and rear-wheel skirts. It was a big, pretty beast, one of the nicest deuce-and-a-quarters on the street. Jones slid into the passenger side and settled on the bench. Jones and Jefferson had first met in the D.C. Jail and, when they could, had worked together since. Jones liked Jefferson's fierce nature, and his style.

Jefferson, small and spidery, looked like a man-child under the wheel. He wore a button-down synthetic shirt, slacks with a wide stripe, and a neat brimmed cap pulled low over his bony face. He had two-tone stacks on his feet. His front teeth were capped in gold. His voice was husky, and he was quick. Johnnie Taylor's "Jody's Got Your Girl and Gone" was playing through an eight-track deck in the car.

"What it is, Red?"

"What it *will* be."

They gave each other skin.

"Got some blondes behind your seat," said Jefferson. "Opener's in the glove box."

Jones retrieved a couple Miller High Lifes, golden in clear glass bottles, and popped their caps. He handed one to Jefferson. Jefferson took a long swig, fitted the bottle between his legs, and pulled off the curb.

*   *   *

ROLAND WILLIAMS lived on T Street, between 13th and 14th, in a house he rented, paying cash, always on time, no references required, no questions asked. The owner of the house was one of several slumlords who had bought run-down properties, pre- and post-riot, and methodically flipped them at an enormous profit to the U.S. government for their "urban renewal" projects. In the late '60s, the practice had been exposed in a series of *Washington Post* articles that had made a splash in the newspaper industry and on Capitol Hill. Reporters won prizes and promotions, but their work had little impact down here; five years later and the area continued to be in the grip of poverty and opportunists.

Williams's row house, on the outside, was as blighted as any other on the block, but inside it was well furnished and nicely appointed. Williams had money. He was the neighborhood heroin dealer, known to most as such, and went untouched and unmolested by the law. Williams paid protection money to Mike Hancock, a Popeye who worked the Third District.

Williams was of the older school of heroin dealer who worked peacefully out of his house. He copped ounces, called "jumbos," at 116th and 8th, up in Harlem. He bought from minor leaguers, black dudes who had scored from Italian button men who were low on the food chain themselves and connected to the Family. The run to Little Baltimore was Williams's pleasure; he liked to go "up top" to the big city, do his thing, eat in one of those nice checkerboard-tablecloth restaurants they had, take his time, drive home slow.

Williams used mannite and quinine to cut his heroin,

which generally was 4 to 12 percent pure when it hit the end user. Four was garbage, 12 a smoker. The temptation was to keep stepping on the dope to maximize profit, but if it was diluted too much a dealer would soon be out of business with a rep for selling trash product. Williams was not greedy, and he was known for delivering an honest kick.

He was a heroin user, but he had that under control. Like many in his line of work, he was functional. He laughed when he saw the TV shows with bad actors in dark-eye-circle makeup, playing strung-out junkies who had fucked up their lives. In Williams's circle, it was macho to be an addict and know how to carry it.

It spoke to a general point of attitude. In his time, criminals were not amateurs. The burglars, car thieves, dope cutters, pickpockets, and flimflam artists he knew were all driven by the skills of their profession and pride in their work. There were few kids in the game. No one realized how soon all this would change.

This last batch of dope he'd copped had not yet been paid for. Williams was short on money at the time of purchase, as he'd recently put a deposit down on a sweet '69 Mark IV that he didn't need but wanted. His contact up top, man named Jimmy Compton, had let him slide because he was a long-time customer in good standing. Williams had brought the product home, cut it down, and packaged it in bundles of twenty-five glassine dime bags. Runners, paid with a shot, would deliver the dimes to residences and places of business. Clients were listed in a book he kept well hidden. Williams had the bundles in paper bags in two locations: the suit carrier in his closet and in a wall cutout behind a hutch in his living room. His intent was to sell the shit, give his New York connect his payment, and add a little bonus to it, to acknowledge the man's trust.

Williams put on some nice threads, as he always did this time of night, and prepared to leave his place for a little something at Soul House, his favorite bar, on 14th. It was a cave, really, just a simple dark room with low music coming from the juke. A spot where he felt comfortable. There he played the role of up-and-coming businessman, sitting at the stick, having himself a quiet drink. Mid-shelf scotch in hand, sometimes with a young lady seated beside him. Thinking, I've made it.

THEY PARKED on the 1300 block of T, drank off a couple more High Lifes, smoked cigarettes, and waited for near dark to come. They were watching a white brick row house with blue shutters, had a little old-time porch on the front. Jefferson had been watching the house for several nights.

"There he goes now," said Jones.

"Told you," said Jefferson. "He leaves out the same time, early in the evening. Goes to that bar, Soul House, on Fourteenth. You can set your watch to it. How they do in London, England, with that big clock they got."

"Roland Williams," said Jones.

"That's Ro-Ro, went to Cardozo?"

Jones shook his head. "*Long Nose* Roland, outta Roosevelt."

"I can see it," said Jefferson.

Roland Williams, with the nose of an aardvark, late twenties, wearing big-bell jeans and a print shirt. He locked the door of the house behind him and walked down the sidewalk.

"Let's go," said Jones.

They got out of the Buick and crossed the street. They came up quick behind Williams, who had turned his head and quickened his step but too late. Jefferson produced an old police-issue .38 with cracked wood grips held fast by electrical tape, and put the barrel of it to the small of Williams's back.

"Keep walkin, slick," said Jefferson. "Straight to the alley."

Williams complied. He moved surely and did not appear to be too shook. They turned into an alley that ran behind Williams's block, uneven stones in concrete, hard beneath their feet.

"Stop and turn around," said Jones. "My man's got his thing on you, so don't be funny."

Williams turned to face them. Somewhere near, a big-breed dog, housed behind a chain-link fence, barked lazily. There was no light back here, save the faint bleed of a streetlamp situated at the end of the alley. It was hard to read Williams's face, but his voice was steady.

"Y'all want my money," said Williams, "go on and take it."

"Give it here," said Jones.

Williams removed folding money from his front pocket and held it out. Jones took it and without examination stuffed it in the patch pocket of his bells.

"Now the key to your crib," said Jones.

"For what?" said Williams.

"'Bout to help myself to your heroin. I know you're holdin."

"Who…"

"Never mind *who*. He kissin dirt." Jones nodded with his chin. "Give it up. I don't want no loose dimes, neither. The bundles."

"You don't understand what you gettin into, brother. I got that shit on consignment."

"Say what?"

"I don't *own* it."

"You got that right. It's mine now."

Williams sighed. They heard his breath expel and saw his shoulders sag.

Jefferson grew impatient and touched his pistol to the man's cheekbone. "Tell him where the dope at."

"What I got is in my bedroom closet," said Williams. "In a suit bag."

"That's it?" said Jones.

"All of it," said Williams. "Swear for God." Williams was a poker player, and they could not read the lie in his eyes.

"Gimme your key."

Jones left the alley with the key to Williams's house and the key to the Buick. Jefferson kept the gun loosely trained on Williams, who calmly lit a cigarette. Neither of them spoke.

Fifteen minutes later, Jones returned. Williams ground the butt under his foot.

"You get it?" said Jefferson.

"Yeah, we're good."

Williams studied them. The tall, light-skinned dude had a distinctive look and a rep to go with it. Had to be Red Jones, who some called Red Fury on account of his woman's car. He knew nothing about the little one with the gold teeth.

"Can I get my house key back?" said Williams.

Jones tossed it in his general direction. Williams did not catch the key, and it fell to the ground with a small pathetic clinking sound. Jones and Jefferson chuckled low.

Williams felt unwise anger rise up inside him. "Y'all motherfuckers ain't gonna last."

"We gonna last longer than you," said Jones, and he drew his .45 from the dip of his bells.

Williams took a staggering step back. Jones moved forward, pressed the gun's muzzle high on Williams's chest, and squeezed its trigger. The night lit up, and in the flash they saw the look of shock on Williams's face as he left his feet and dropped to the alley floor. Blood pooled out from Williams's back. His chest heaved up as he fought for breath. Then his eyes closed and he moved no more.

"Next time," said Jefferson, "gimme some kind of warning. My ears are ringin, Red."

"Boy talked too much shit."

They left him for dead. It was a mistake.

FIVE

STRANGE HAD traded in his Impala and bought a low-mileage, triple-black, '70 Monte Carlo from the Curtis Chevrolet at Georgia and Missouri. He'd be paying on it for three years, but he had no buyer's remorse. He was a GM man who was working his way up to a Cadillac, but for now he was more than satisfied. The lines were extra clean, with rally rims, Goodyear radials, and a small-block 350 under the hood. The interior had sweet buckets, a horseshoe shifter on the console, factory eight-track sound, and a wood-grain dash. It was a pretty car.

Strange drove it downtown, Curtis's *Roots* in the deck, "Get Down" playing loud.

He found a parking spot and commenced to knocking on doors in the apartment building at 13th and R, where Bobby Odum had lived. He began on the top floor and got very little in the way of leads. He was a young black man, casually but not loudly dressed, nice looking and well built, with a polite manner. Most important, he was not the law. So the residents of the building, for the most part, talked to him freely. But the information he received held little value in terms of his quest. He was looking for a ring, not Bobby Odum's killer. Homicide was police business and always had been. Private detectives only solved murders in movies and dime novels.

On the bottom floor, he found a young woman named Janette Newman, a compact, nicely put-together gal who had the Marcus Garvey thing going on in her apartment. She let him in, offered him a seat on the sofa, and served him a soda. He learned that she was a schoolteacher at Harriet Tubman and that she was single.

"You live here alone?"

"Most nights," she said.

"I imagine you saw the comings and goings of Bobby Odum. He had visitors, right?"

"There was this one light-skinned girl."

"Speak to her?"

"She wasn't the approachable type."

"Ever rap with Odum?"

"Sometimes. He had a job, and in the morning we'd leave here around the same time."

"So you know where he worked at."

"He washed dishes at that fish place up on Georgia," she said. "Cobb's?"

"I know the spot."

"Walked over to Seventh and took the uptown bus, every day."

"I assume you told all this to the homicide detective who came to see you. Vaughn, right?"

"Big white dude. Don't recall his name. I wasn't about to tell that man too much. They never do anything for us, anyway. *You* know how that is."

Strange nodded. He had identified himself as a self-employed investigator. He had not told her that he was former MPD.

"I hope I'm being of help." She parted her lips and smiled.

It was a fetching smile, but there was little warmth to it, and no kindness in her eyes. He imagined she could run to mean sometimes, too.

Strange liked all kinds of women. They didn't have to be beautiful to catch his attention, but they did have to be nice. His girlfriend, Carmen, was both.

He had not always been faithful to her, but he knew what he had.

"Anything else I can do for you?" said Janette.

"Not today," said Strange.

Outside the building, Strange saw a man sitting on a retaining wall and doing nothing. Looked like a guy who lived on the streets. If this was his spot, he was the type of person who would notice things, that is if he was not too high. Strange took steps toward him. The man watched him dolefully, then got off the wall and walked away. Strange went to his car.

THE CARRYOUT on the west side of Georgia, in Park View, specialized in fish sandwiches. Case no one knew, the sign out front, featuring a big old bass leaping out of the water with a hook and line in its mouth, announced it. Strange asked the owner, Ordell Cobb, for a minute of his time. Cobb was in his fifties and wore an apron smudged with ketchup and blood. His manner was gruff. They were at the rear of the kitchen, near a door leading to an alley, workers hustling around them. The stainless steel sink that Odum had most likely stood over, its power nozzle hanging above, sat right beside them. WOL was playing on the house radio. Strange knew, 'cause Bobby "the Mighty Burner" Bennett was introducing a song.

"I already told the white detective," said Cobb. "I don't know nothin about Odum's murder. He washed dishes for me, is all. I don't get into the personal lives of my employees."

"You owe him any back pay?"

"Why?"

"Tryin to see if any relatives or friends of his dropped by."

"He owed *me* money, on a *ad*vance I gave him."

"One more thing: you notice if he was ever wearing a ring, had a big cluster of stones on it?"

Cobb shook his head in exasperation. "I didn't study on him all that much. Look, young man, I gotta get back to work."

"Okay, then. Let me get a couple of fish sandwiches for takeaway before I get out of here."

"The flounder or the trout?"

"Make it the trout," said Strange. "Extra hot sauce."

Kinda counterproductive, thought Strange, as Cobb moved toward the deep-fry basket. Me and Vaughn covering the same ground.

STRANGE TOOK the sandwiches over to his mother's row house at 760 Princeton Place, his childhood home. His father,

Darius, had passed a couple of years earlier from cancer, and his older brother, Dennis, had been murdered by a low criminal just before the riots. The losses had set his mother back emotionally, but the deaths of her loved ones had not broken her. Alethea Strange was a woman of faith, and she still had her younger son.

It was a Saturday, so Strange knew she would be home. Monday through Friday she worked as a receptionist for a downtown ophthalmologist who serviced the shirt-and-tie class. The eye doctor was a former client whose home she had cleaned for many years. He offered her a job in his office in April 1968, after she told him that she would no longer be doing domestic work of any kind. The man thought of himself as a liberal in matters of race, whatever that meant, and he had probably hired her out of guilt, because she had no experience for the position. But his internal motives made no difference to her. She took to the work quickly and did her job well.

Alethea greeted Strange at the door with a delighted smile. He tried to phone her once a day, but, like many sons who meant well, he did not get over to her place as much as he intended to.

"I brought some Cobb's, Mama," said Strange, holding up a brown paper bag darkened with grease.

They ate in the living room, where Strange used to roughhouse with Dennis, sometimes just wrestling, sometimes full-out boxing, his father amused, sitting in his chair, reading the Washington edition of the *Afro-American*, listening to his Sam Cooke and Jackie Wilson records on the console, or watching Westerns on his Zenith TV, or talking about that awful man who owned the Redskins and local-products-gone-pro like Elgin Baylor and Maury Wills. Strange had his father's albums in his own collection now, but the console stereo was still here, being used mostly as a stand for his mother's potted violets.

The place looked the same, a small living area, two bedrooms, a galley kitchen, even the wall decorations were the same, but it was too quiet, the only noise coming from the longtime tenants on the first floor. Made Strange sad to visit, thinking how still it must be when it was just his mother here.

"This is good," said Alethea, closing her eyes as she swallowed.

"I went for the trout," said Strange.

After, they moved to the kitchen, where she finished up the dishes she'd been washing when he had arrived. The window over the sink had cardboard taped to its bottom pane. Alethea did this so as not to disturb the babies in the nest built by robins on the outdoor sill every spring.

He watched her as she worked in her housedress. She still had a younger woman's figure, but she listed a bit, favoring the hip that did not ache. Seated behind an office desk, answering phones and dealing with patients, was not physically demanding, but the time his mother had spent as a maid had taken its toll on her knees and back. She had aged ten years in the past four; in the final months of Darius's painful illness, her hair had gone completely gray as she tended to her husband in their home.

"How's Carmen?" she said, looking slightly over her shoulder.

"Good. We're going to a movie tonight."

"Don't be takin her to one of your Westerns."

"What you want me to do, go to some weepy?"

"Make her happy, Derek."

"Yes, ma'am."

Strange leaned against the Formica counter, his arms crossed, watching her work, listening to her hum. When she was done, she dried her hands and hung the towel on a rod.

"Thank you for stopping by, son."

"My pleasure," said Strange.

HE WAS done working for the day, and he had some time to kill, so he drove farther north on Georgia and stopped at a place called the Experience for a beer. It was a small joint, just a room with a steel-top bar front to back, a few tables, and a jukebox. The juke stayed mostly unplugged, on account of the owner, young dude named Grady Page, liked to play funk-rock music, the hybrid thing he loved, through the house system. The Experience was a neighborhood spot, had posters thumbtacked to its walls. It catered to a mix of local drinkers, heads, off-duty police officers, utility workers, security guards, and women who liked men who wore uniforms.

Strange had a seat at the bar next to a snaggletoothed MPD patrolman, Harold Cheek, out of 4-D, who was in streetclothes today. Funkadelic's "You Hit the Nail on the Head" was on the system, the lead track off their latest, George Clinton playing his Hammond wild and free, a speed freak's idea of a circus tent song. Grady Page liked to spin the new.

"Gimme a Bud, Grady," said Strange. Page, tall and lean, was going for the unofficial Biggest Afro in D.C. award. He reached into the cooler.

"You see Grady?" said Cheek with amusement. "Tryin to look like Darnell Hillman and shit."

"Artis Gilmore got a big 'Fro, too," said Strange.

"Not as big as Darnell's."

Strange was served. With one deep swig he drank the shoulders off the Bud.

"Heard your man Lydell got his stripes," said Cheek.

"Yeah, Lydell's doin all right."

Lydell Blue, Strange's main boy from their Park View youth, had entered the MPD academy at the same time as Strange and had recently been promoted to sergeant. An army regular with time served in Vietnam, he had recently married a girl he'd met at his church. Strange felt Lydell had pulled the trigger too young, but realized that it was he, and not his friend, who was not ready.

"Y'all played football together at Roosevelt, right?" said Cheek.

"I went both ways," said Strange. "Tight end and safety. Lydell was a fullback. Mostly, I tried to open the field up for him."

"He had the Interhigh record for yardage gained, didn't he?"

"His senior year. Lydell could play."

Cheek looked him over. "You miss it?"

"Football?"

"The *force*."

"I don't miss it at all,' said Strange. "They sure don't need me. Not with heroes like you out there."

"Go *ahead*, Derek."

"You know Vaughn, don't you? Homicide police?"

"I know *of* him."

"Where's he out of now?"

"Last I heard, Three-D."

An off-duty security guard named Frank came over and greeted them with soul shakes. "What it look like, brothers?"

"Frank," said Cheek.

Frank was good natured and had a pleasant face. He was wearing big bells with a wide brown belt and a knit shirt holding horizontal stripes. Real police sometimes called security guards "scarecrows" or "counterfeit cops," especially the ones who weren't much more than migrant workers, passing through town on their way to someplace else. But no one cracked on Frank, a local with a work ethic. Two oh five an hour, and he did his job straight.

"Where he guarding at now?" said Strange, after Frank had drifted.

"He's down at that big hotel complex in Foggy Bottom. One on Virginia Avenue?"

"Frank's cool," said Strange.

A couple of ladies visited. One of them, a nice little deep-dark girl who was put together right, offered to get Strange high, and they went out back to the alley, where she produced a number and fired it up. Grady Page joined them for a minute. He and Strange shotgunned each other, then Strange did the same for the girl, whose name was LaVonya. Page went back inside to do his thing. LaVonya said to Strange, "You're a big one," and he said, "You should see me when I stand up," and though he was already standing and the comment made no sense, it sounded funny, and the two of them laughed. She wrote down her phone number and Strange took it, because he was a man, and as soon as they went back into the bar he lost track of her.

Page was playing the title cut off *The World Is a Ghetto*, the long version from the brand-new War, and Strange was higher than a Denver hippie as he drank another beer, the instrumental middle of the song building emotionally, almost violently, taking him up, Strange knowing that he was young and in the midst of something, a music, dress, and cultural revolution that was happening with his people, in his time. Where it was going he had no clue, but he was glad to be a part of it.

"Man, you are trippin," said Cheek with a chuckle. He had returned to his spot beside Strange, who had not noticed he was gone. "Where LaVonya at?"

"Who?"

"You better have another beer to straighten your shit out."

"Okay, then," said Strange. "And one for you. On me."

Grady Page, smiling absently, up-picking his hair with his rake, had a power fist as a handle, was leaning against the beer cooler. Strange held up two fingers and signaled for one more round.

WHEN STRANGE woke up, in the bedroom of his apartment on the northeast corner of 13th and Clifton, dusk had come. A nap was what he had needed, and it had cleared his head. He showered and changed into clean clothes, and soon Carmen knocked on his door.

She was in pale slacks, cork-wedge shoes, and a pretty

lilac-colored shirt that played off nice against her dark skin. She wore her hair in a natural, and when she smiled her deep dimples showed. He'd been knowing her since they were kids, and reckoned that he'd loved her just as long.

They kissed.

"What's goin on, baby?"

"Oh, I don't know. I've been calling you to firm up our plans."

"I fell asleep. Guess I didn't hear the phone."

"Thought you were working today."

"I *was*," said Strange, frowning as if accused. "Workin *all* the time. Even when I sleep, I work."

"Go on, Derek." Carmen smiled. "What are we gonna see tonight?"

"*Culpepper Cattle Company*?"

"Please."

"I'm playing with you." But he really did want to see it.

"What about *Georgia, Georgia*? It's playing at the Langston."

"All the way in Northeast?"

"Benning Road's not far."

"What's it about?"

"Diana Sands plays this singer, falls in love with an army deserter in Sweden."

"Might as well give me a sleeping pill instead."

"So? You tryin to take me to a cow movie."

"Cow*boy*."

"Same thing, to me."

"How about this? I got some of that wine you like in the

fridge. Let's have a glass or two, then go out and catch a little dinner."

She walked toward him. "I guess we could."

Strange put *Al Green Gets Next to You* on his stereo and poured some Blue Nun as "Are You Lonely for Me Baby" set the mood. It was Al's deep-soul record, full of grit and fire. They drank the too-sweet white by the open French doors on the south wall, Carmen sitting close to him, his arm around her shoulders as they talked about their day, looking down on the city lights below. His place was on the edge of the Piedmont Plateau, a low-rent district, but no rich man had a better view of D.C.

"You hungry?" said Strange.

"Not really."

"Come here, girl."

STRANGE WOKE naked in his bed. Carmen, nude atop the sheets, was sleeping beside him. Though they had made love twice that evening, the sight of her body made his mouth go dry. She'd been working toward medical school, but financial issues had steered her to nursing. Now an RN at the Columbia Hospital for Women, she had the beginnings of a solid, meaningful career. He was proud of Carmen and, despite his failings, wanted to do her right. He covered her, put on his drawers, and left the bedroom.

He went to the living room, where soul records were scattered around his stereo, his expensive Marantz tube amplifier the center of the space. On the wall was an original one-sheet poster of the Man With No Name, tall in his poncho, a prize possession that Strange had gotten from a friend who'd worked at the Town theater on 13th and New York Avenue. Also, a Jim Brown lobby still from *The Dirty Dozen*, copped from the same dude. Wasn't any mistaking it: a man lived here.

Strange picked up the phone, dialed the number for the Third District station, and got the desk man on the line. He gave the sergeant his home and office numbers, and left a message for Frank Vaughn.

SIX

"Can I get that cup, Detective?"

Vaughn lifted a plastic cup off a tray and put it in Roland Williams's outstretched hand. Williams sipped water from a straw that was hinged at a ninety-degree angle. He ran his tongue over his dry lips and kept the cup in hand.

"You had some luck," said Vaughn.

"Do I look lucky to you?"

Williams, weak and thin, was in a hospital bed in D.C. General, hooked up to an IV, his shoulder and arm in a blue sling, bandages and dressing beneath it. The slug had entered his upper chest and exited cleanly through his back, so the close-range shot had been a kind of blessing.

Williams's luck was not of the lottery-winning variety, or that of an ugly man going home with the prettiest girl in the bar, but it was something to be thankful for.

"Tell us what happened," said Rick Cochnar, the young man who was standing beside Vaughn. He did not look like many of the assistant prosecutors in his office. He was state school educated, with longish hair and the build of a full-back. He was short, with big hands. He was wearing a charcoal-colored suit with thin chalk stripes.

Williams turned his head and looked at his attorney, Tim Doyle, a Jesuit school graduate and baseball-playing stand-out in his day, now in love with drink. He was seated in the guest chair of the room.

"You have immunity," said Doyle with a small nod.

"What about—"

"That's inadmissible."

The police on the scene had found Williams's house key in the alley beside his unconscious body. A bystander had identified Williams and his place of residence. Uniformed police, under the supervision of an overly ambitious sergeant, used the key to enter the house, searched the place thoroughly, and found a large amount of bundled heroin in a false wall behind a hutch. They had no warrant and no PC.

"I'm homicide police," said Vaughn. "I don't give a rat's ass about heroin."

"Who did this to you?" said Cochnar.

Williams took another drink of water and let a silence settle in the room. "I'm damn near sure the man goes by Red."

"Last name?" said Vaughn.

"Jones."

"Does Red have a Christian name?"

"I expect he does, unless he popped out the devil's ass."

"What else do you know about Jones?"

Williams paused. Over the ghetto telegraph he'd heard that Red Jones had a woman named Coco, ran a trick-house on 14th, near R, over a market once owned by a Jew, now run by a Rican. But there wasn't any good reason to spill that information here. He'd already said too much.

"I don't know nothin else," said Williams.

Vaughn nodded. The name Red Jones was enough. Vaughn had already narrowed Reds-with-rap-sheets down to three. A .45 shell casing carrying a partial print had been recovered from the alley. Jones would have priors and prints on file. Now Vaughn would have to find someone to squeeze. Roland Williams, in exchange for speaking off the record with Vaughn and Cochnar, would not be required to testify. Vaughn didn't want Jones for an *attempted* murder, anyway. He wanted him on the murder of Odum.

"Describe Jones," said Vaughn.

Williams gave them detailed descriptions of Red Jones and his accomplice, whose name he did not know. Cochnar wrote it down, and Vaughn committed it to memory.

"You're Homicide," said Williams. "So why you here? Ain't nobody murder me."

"This isn't about you," said Vaughn. "You told your lawyer that you think there's a connection between this Red character and a case I'm currently working. The victim was Robert Odum."

Again, Williams glanced at his attorney.

"Go ahead," said Doyle.

"I got robbed, Detective," said Williams. "Man took my money and somethin else that belonged to me. Bobby Odum was an associate of mine, the only man in town who knew what I had in my possession."

"You've got runners, don't you?"

"My runners know what I got when I'm ready to tell 'em. Bobby was a tester. He knew I had product before anyone else did. Had to be Odum who gave me up."

Cochnar was taking notes in a book of lined paper he held in hand. Williams was watching him.

"I ain't tryin to dead myself," said Williams. "I'll plead the Fifth, I have to."

"The detective's already been informed," said Doyle.

"Where'd you get the dope?" said Vaughn.

"Harlem," said Williams.

"You copped from brothers?"

"Through the Family."

"The Italians aren't gonna like this."

"That's what I *know*. When I get out of here, I plan to give this life up, for real."

"Sure you will." Vaughn looked down at Roland, his honker coming out of his gaunt face like the pecker of an aroused dog. "They call you Long Nose, don't they?"

"Some do," said Williams defensively.

"I can see it," said Vaughn, and showed Williams his row of widely spaced teeth. "Take care of yourself."

Vaughn and Cochnar left the room. Walking down the busy hallway, they discussed the case. Cochnar had been in charge of prosecuting a James Carpenter, awaiting trial in the D.C. Jail on a homicide, when Odum was killed. Cochnar suspected that Carpenter had ordered the hit on Odum because he believed that Odum had provided information that led to Carpenter's arrest. Vaughn and Cochnar now liked Red Jones for that murder-for-hire.

They passed a tall, chiseled, uniformed security guard

who worked for a private company under contract with the hospital. His name was Clarence Bowman, and he had been raised in an alley dwelling known as Temperance Court.

Bowman followed Vaughn and Cochnar out to the parking lot, RFK Stadium and the D.C. Armory looming over the landscape. He kept well behind them so he would not be noticed. The big white man got into a large Dodge sedan. He looked like police, so that was no surprise. The stocky white boy in the suit unlocked a shiny pea-green Ford Maverick and settled into the driver's side. Young dude with his first real job out of law school, driving his first new car. Cochnar, the government prosecutor. Had to be.

STRANGE SAT on 13th in his Monte Carlo, listening to the radio, waiting. He was hoping that the man he had seen the day before would reappear. It wasn't just a blind man's grope. Street people had their favorite spots and seldom changed locations until chased off.

He was there a half hour or so when the man came out of an apartment building across the street from Odum's. The man used the crosswalk, went to the retaining wall that was his chair, and had a seat on the edge of it, his feet dangling over the sidewalk. Strange got out of his car.

The man did not move as Strange approached, nor did he look away. Strange came up on him, his arms loose, his stance unthreatening, and stood before him.

"Afternoon," said Strange. "I was hoping we could talk."

Up close, the man's eyes were not unintelligent, nor were they the empty eyes of a dope fiend, but he looked beaten. Though it was warm out, he wore an old-style cardigan sweater over a shirt with a frayed collar. His hair was shaved close to the scalp with a slash part, a barbershop cut from ten years back. The slope of his shoulders and his folded arms suggested surrender.

"You police?"

"Not anymore. I'm private. My name's Derek Strange. Can I buy you a beer, something?"

"I don't drink. You got a smoke?"

"Sorry."

The man bit his lip as something came to mind. "I knew a Strange. Boy named Dennis. Older than you, about your size."

"Dennis was my brother."

"We used to hang out some, at house parties and all, before he joined the navy. I heard he passed. My sympathies, man."

"Thank you."

The man put his hand out and Strange shook it. "Milton Wallace."

"Pleasure," said Strange. "You served, too?"

"Army," said Wallace, and then Strange knew. This wasn't any street person, or drunk, or junkie. The man was a veteran who'd been in it and come out torn on the other side.

Strange looked up at the sky. Raindrops had begun to fall and more were on the way. "We should get out of this."

"I live with my mother in that building," said Wallace, pointing to the door from which he'd exited. "But I don't want to disturb her."

"My Chevy's right over there."

Wallace smiled wistfully. "That's a pretty MC."

*   *   *

THE NEW Stylistics song, "People Make the World Go Round," was on the radio and playing low, Russell Thompkins Jr.'s angelic vocals an apt, melodic narration to the life they were seeing, tableau-form, through the windshield. On 13th, a tired woman shuffled down the sidewalk, carrying a bag of groceries. A group of young girls double-Dutched on the corner, and on a nearby stoop a man was pleading with a woman, gesturing elaborately with his hands to make his case.

"City ain't all that different since I been back," said Wallace. "Little burned around the edges, maybe. But still the same rough old ghetto."

"You missed the trouble."

"I had my own troubles to worry on."

"Where were you?"

"Bao Loc, mostly. Northeast of Saigon. I was with Charlie Company, the One Seventy-Third."

Strange had heard tell of the company. Lydell had occasionally invoked its name with reverence.

"You?" said Wallace.

"My knee kept me out. Football injury."

"You oughta thank the one who put the hurtin on you."

"I reckon I should," said Strange. "You see much action?"

Wallace did not reply. As it was for many veterans, his combat experience was sacred to him and the men he had fought with. He had no intention of discussing it with this young man.

"What's this about?" said Wallace.

"I wanted to talk to you about the Odum murder."

"Figured as much. But we gonna have to settle on something first."

"I don't have any money to speak of."

"It's not about coin. I'll talk to you but no one else. And if you put the police on me, I'll deny I told you anything."

"The law can protect you."

"I'm not afraid. But my mother lost a leg to diabetes, and now she's confined to a chair. She needs me, man. Understand?"

"You have my word," said Strange. "Did the police question you?"

"A white detective tried to give me money and liquor in exchange for conversation. Like I was some kind of bum."

"You knew Odum?"

"Not really. Seen him on the street now and then."

"Were you over there on that wall at the time of the killing?"

"There every day."

"And?"

"The music got my attention, comin from this apartment on the second floor. It was soft at first, then real loud. And then, under it, a little pop. Small-caliber gun. Few minutes later, a tall light-skinned dude with a fucked-up natural come out the building, walkin like nothing happened. He went to a car."

"What kind of car?"

"Late-model Fury, red over white. Had the fold-in headlamps. A woman with big hair or a wig was behind the wheel. The tall man got in the passenger side."

"He see you?"

"If he did, he didn't much care."

"I'm looking for a ring was in Odum's possession the time of his death. Wonderin maybe if the tall man had it in hand when he walked to the Plymouth."

"Shit." Wallace chuckled. "Now you expectin me to know too much."

"I took a swing at it."

"You on a treasure hunt, huh."

"Somethin like that."

"Plenty of police went in and out of Odum's crib. Might could be one of them took that ring."

"I thought of that."

"Or you just gonna have to ask the tall dude yourself."

"Hoping to avoid that if I can," said Strange. "What else about the car? You didn't get the plate number, did you?"

"Wasn't no numbers," said Wallace. "Plate was the kind had words on it."

"You remember what it said?"

"Coco," said Wallace. "C-O, C-O."

"D.C. tags?"

"Right."

Strange experienced a small familiar rush. All the bullshit jobs he'd taken for money lately, it had been a while since he had been involved in something real.

"You got strong observation skills," said Strange. "What do you do for work?"

"I don't do a thing."

"You can't find a job?"

"Can't keep one. Man at the VA says I got problems. Emotional stress brought on by my 'intense experience overseas.' Says time gonna heal me."

"Maybe he's right."

"Truth, is, I don't know *what* to do. So I sit." Wallace smiled a little, catching a memory. "Your brother Dennis was a funny dude. We laughed like crazy in the day."

"He was good."

Dennis had been found in the alley behind their boyhood home, his throat cut open with a knife. He'd been butchered like an animal.

But I took care of the one who did it, thought Strange. *Me and Vaughn.*

"Thanks for this." Strange put out his hand.

SEVEN

LOU FANELLA and Gino Gregorio had come down from New-ark on the Turnpike, taking the BW Parkway south into D.C. They entered the city via New York Avenue in a black '69 Continental sedan with suicide doors and a 460 V-8.

"What a shithole," said Fanella, big and beefy, with dark hair and Groucho eyebrows. His thick wrist rested on the wheel as he drove, a cigarette burning between his fingers.

He was looking at the run-down gateway to Washington that was the first impression for many visitors to the nation's capital, a mix of warehouses, liquor stores, unadorned bars, and rank motels housing criminals, prostitutes, last-stop drunks, and welfare families.

"This is where Zoot said to rent a room?" said Fanella.

"That's what he said." Gregorio was on the young side, with a wiry build, thinning blond hair, the cool blue eyes of an Italian horse opera villain, and a face cratered with scars grimly memorializing the nightmarish acne of his adolescence.

"It's all smokes 'round here," said Fanella.

"There were some places looked all right, back where we were."

"Then let's go back to where we were."

They turned around and got a room in a motel off Kenilworth Avenue, in Prince George's County, Maryland. Their room smelled strongly of bleach and faintly of puke. The area itself was no better than the one they had rejected, but most of the people here were white. Now they were comfortable.

They went out and bought liquor and mixers and brought the goods back to the room. Fanella drank Ten High bourbon and Gregorio went with Seagram's 7. *The Black Shield of Falworth* was playing on their small television set, and they watched the swords-and-tights movie while they drank and put away cigarettes. Soon the room was heavy with smoke and the sound of their thoughtful conversation.

"Janet Leigh," said Fanella. "*God.*" He shook the ice in his glass and looked at Gregorio. "Tony Curtis is a Jew. Did you know that?"

"So?"

"Means Janet likes her salami cut."

"I'm like that down there, too."

"Yeah, but you don't look like Tony. I bet he had that dish up one side and down the other all day long."

"How would you know?"

" 'Cause he was married to her, you dumbass."

"Oh."

"*Look* at that. I love it when a broad has a narrow waist and big tits. How about you, Gino?"

"I guess."

"You guess?"

"Who doesn't?"

"Homos," said Fanella.

They found a place nearby that had steaks on special and a salad bar. After the main they went with a couple of slices of cheesecake, then settled up the check and drove back into the city. They found Thomas "Zoot" Mazzetti seated at the bar of a place called the Embers, on the 1200 block of 19th Street.

A jazzy outfit called the Frank Hinton Group was playing in the lounge for an audience of lawyers, lawyer types, and secretaries, all dressed nice, seated around the low-lit spot. Fanella and Gregorio wore sport jackets and polyester slacks with bold-print shirts, collars out over the lapels. They looked like what they were.

Fanella felt that Zoot was showing off, setting the meeting at a high-end spot. Like, look at me; I have made it. Zoot had come up in their area and like them had worked for the Organization on the ladder's lowest rungs. All of them were high school dropouts. Gino Gregorio, at the bottom of the bell curve, had done a stint in the army but had gone no further than the motor pool.

Years earlier, Zoot had followed a girl south to the Baltimore–Washington corridor. She soon threw him over for a guy with a brain and a job. By then Zoot had grown comfortable with the area. He was a novelty here, a real Italian just like Pacino instead of another failed swinging dick from the neighborhood back home. He decided to stay and found a niche in D.C. as a bookie and a buyer and seller of information. Lately he had developed a relationship with a local cop who was into him on a gambling debt for two thousand dollars and change. Zoot was not book smart but he knew how to operate.

"Big shot," said Fanella. "Look at you."

Zoot smiled, stepped back from the bar, let them see his getup, tight jeans with a dollar-sign belt buckle, a rayon shirt, and a cinnamon-colored leather jacket.

"Them pants are kinda snug, ain't they?" said Fanella, winking at Gregorio.

"That's for the ladies," said Zoot. "I dress to the left, as you can see."

"You look like a hairdresser," said Fanella.

"Fuck you and buy me a drink."

They had cocktails and got around to why they had come. Zoot told them where they could find Roland Williams, the man they were looking for. He said the information had come from a law enforcement officer he had "on retainer" and the tip was golden. For his trouble they picked up the tab but gave Zoot nothing extra. It was understood that he was still connected, however tenuously, to the outfit, and always would be.

"Where can we look at some women in this town?" said Fanella. "You know what I'm talking about. Ann-Margret types."

Zoot gave them a suggestion.

Fanella and Gregorio went down to the Gold Rush, a burlesque club low on 14th. No cover, no minimum. Daphne Lake and her "exotic revue" were performing. Daphne's protégées were double-D gals with plenty of flank and ass, but, to the disappointment and annoyance of Fanella, they showed no wool. Disoriented in their new surroundings, they walked the streets and came upon a theater, the Playhouse, showing a stroke picture called *Bacchanale*. "You must see Uta Erickson!" it said on the marquee, and they bit. Sitting there in the auditorium with the raincoat creeps who were moaning as they jacked off into newspapers and socks. It was distracting, but eventually Fanella's trousers got tight, and he went to the bathroom and rubbed one off in the privacy of a stall. Returning to his seat, he tugged on Gregorio's jacket and told him it was time to go.

"The movie's not finished," said Gregorio.

"Foreign pictures stink," said Fanella. "Come on."

The Lincoln was where they'd left it, around the corner from the Gold Rush. Fanella cruised out of town, careful to stay within ten miles of the speed limit. He had a switchblade with a bone handle in his pocket. Under the driver's seat was a loaded .38. In the trunk were two cut-down shotguns and slings, handguns of various calibers, bricks of ammunition, a baseball bat, a pair of lead-filled saps, a set of butcher knives wrapped in soft cloth, and a white raincoat. Fanella did not want to have to shoot a police officer over a traffic stop. His people would not like it if he went to jail before completing his task. He and Gino had work to do.

ROBERT LEE Jones was seated in the chair beside the red velvet couch where Shirley "Coco" Watkins lounged in her office, drinking pink champagne, enjoying a Viceroy. Her new ring was in a silverware box under the bed, where she kept her jewelry. Jones was having King George scotch cut with a little bit of water. In the rooms down the hall, Coco's girls were working.

"Time for me to move out," said Jones. "Gonna room with Alfonzo for a while over in Burrville. I can't be stayin here."

"For real?"

"I'm too hot."

"You the one lit the stove."

"You see me sweatin?"

"I never have before."

"I'm not stressed. I got cash now, Coco. Couple a thousand. Fonzo offed the product wholesale and we split the take."

"You woulda made more, you sold it by the piece."

"I got no interest in heroin. Just money."

"So if you're flush, what's your problem? You got a bed right here."

"People been seein us together. I ain't about to wait for the law to show up. Me and Fonzo got a chance to make some real coin now."

Jones produced a pack of Kools from his breast pocket, flipped it, and extracted a menthol out of the hole he had torn in the bottom of the deck. He lit it with a match from the Ed Murphy's Supper Club book he had taken from Odum's apartment.

"What are y'all's plans?" said Coco.

"We're goin at Sylvester Ward."

"Two-Tone Ward? The numbers man?"

"Him. Fonzo been sittin on him and knows his routine."

"Shit. You gonna take off Ward now."

"Because we can."

She blinked demurely. There was esteem and affection in her gaze. Also, concern for her man.

"You gettin bold," she said.

"My name's ringing out in this town," said Jones. "People talkin about me in barbershops, on the stoops. Young motherfuckers steppin aside when I walk into the club. They all wanna be like me."

"More you get known, bigger chance you gonna get taken down."

"Then I'll go down," said Jones.

"What about us?"

"You're my bottom, girl."

He leaned forward and kissed her full mouth. He put his hand behind her neck to keep her in. Her tongue snaked around his. Sometimes her mouth was as good as her box, to him. Sometimes.

"How you fixin to cool things down?" said Coco.

"I made a mistake with Roland Williams. He's in D.C. General right now, but when he comes out? I'm gonna take care of it. My man from back home will see to some other problems we got, too." Jones double-dragged on his cigarette, let the smoke out slow. "What's your girl's name, got the mark on her face?"

"That's a mole, Red. You talkin about Shay."

"She been hangin with that dude come out of Lorton premature. Right?"

"Dallas Butler. You had a drink with him yourself, right here in this room."

"*Dallas*, yeah. Boy's custard. What was he in for?"

"He was doing sixteen on an armed robbery when he busted out."

"We gonna make him a murderer, too. But I'm gonna need your help."

Coco stubbed her Viceroy out in the ashtray after a hungry last drag. "What you want me to do?"

"Ask Shay to hook up a meet. Tell her I want to talk to her boy, but I want it to be a surprise. Not so she'd have cause to be suspicious. You know how to do it. Me and Fonzo will take care of the rest."

"Anything else?"

"Pick up the phone," said Jones.

He gave her instructions. She dialed the Third District station house and asked for Detective Vaughn. The voice on the other end of the line told her Vaughn was not in.

"Let me leave a message, then."

"What's your name and location?"

"Never mind that," said Coco. "This about the Robert Odum murder, over there at Thirteenth and R. I know who downed the dude. The killer's name is Dallas Butler. Dallas like the football team, Butler how it sounds."

She hung up the phone.

Jones smiled and got up out of his seat. "You did good."

"Where you goin?"

"Out."

"Don't forget about the show. It's comin up."

"What show's that?"

"Donny and Roberta at the Carter Barron. You copped the tickets, fool!"

"Oh, yeah." He wasn't excited about it. Music for females and pretty boys. It was weak.

"Come here."

He bent into her kiss. Standing to his full height, he patted the side of his unkempt natural and let her admire him.

"I'll be around, Coco."

"I know you will."

EIGHT

FRANK VAUGHN and Derek Strange sat at a lunch counter on Vermont Avenue owned and operated by a Greek named Nick. The diner seated twenty-seven: fifteen stools covered in blue vinyl and three blue vinyl booths that each fit four. Old photographs of the village were hung on the blue-and-white tiled walls, as well as formal-suit portraits of the owner's immigrant parents. Near the front door stood a D.C. Vending cigarette machine with copies of the *Daily News* tabloid set upon it. Beside the machine was a pay phone.

Nick Michael was born Nick Michaelopoulos in Sparta, came to America as a toddler, and was a veteran of the infamous Battle of Peleliu in the Pacific theater. Like many marines who had fought, Nick had settled into a peaceful life of hard work during the day and quiet relaxation at night. He had shot and bayoneted many Japanese soldiers, and seen the deaths of many friends, but except for the USMC tattoo on his inner forearm, there was nothing about his manner or appearance to suggest his violent war experience. He had come out of the Corps at a lean 145, was now fifty-one years old, went 180, and had a respectable paunch that was slightly visible beneath his apron. He sported a full head of hair, black on top, silver on the sides, and a pleasant, confident smile.

"Anything else I can do you for?" said Nick.

"You can warm up these coffees," said Vaughn.

Nick put his hands around Vaughn's cup and, with great exaggeration, rubbed it. "How's this?"

"That gag's got gray hair on it," said Vaughn.

"Like us."

Nick picked up their cups and saucers, went to one of his big urns, flipped down the black valve-style lever, and poured fresh coffee. He served Vaughn and Strange, emptied Vaughn's ashtray, and put it back in front of him. Vaughn promptly lit an L&M with his Zippo and placed the lighter atop his newly opened pack.

"I like this place," said Vaughn.

"It's all right," said Strange.

They had just eaten a breakfast of scrapple and eggs. The food was on the bland side by design, as the diner catered to white-collar whites. The crew behind the counter, hot station, cold station, waitress, and dishwasher, were black. The woman working hots had fried some onions and pepper into the eggs for Strange and he had further spiced up the plate with Tabasco. Strange's father had been a grill man for the Three-Star, a place on Kennedy Street very much like this one. Darius Strange had also worked for a Greek, Mike Georgelakos, who had dropped dead of a massive heart attack in 1969.

"So you're looking for a ring," said Vaughn.

"Maybelline Walker's. You met her."

"Nice-looking lady. Teacher, I recall."

"She's a math tutor."

"Right." Vaughn dragged on his cigarette. "I don't think she cared much for me. I wouldn't let her look around Odum's apartment."

"She had a key. Let herself in after y'all closed the scene."

"The resourceful type. What's so special about the ring?"

"Has sentimental value, she says. Costume jewelry. Says she and Odum were friends. Odum was gonna get the ring assessed for her, to see if it had any value. Stones were a cluster of glass but the body of it was gold. *She* says."

"You don't believe her."

"She hired me to find the ring. Don't much care about the why." Strange looked at Vaughn, who was exhaling a thin stream of smoke over the Formica-covered counter. "You didn't happen to see it, did you?"

"A ring? No. There was some women's jewelry we found in his bedroom dresser. A bracelet and a necklace, too, if I remember right."

"Real shit?"

"I wouldn't know. Bobby used to do Burglary Ones, years ago. Said he lost his ambition after he fell in love with smack. Maybe the trinkets in the bedroom were some old pieces he was holding on to."

"What happened to that jewelry?"

"Property's got it," said Vaughn. "You think Odum's killer took the ring?"

"Or one of the uniforms on the scene slipped it in his pocket."

"It happens. But I'd put money on the one who chilled Odum."

"You got a suspect?"

Vaughn showed Strange his choppers. "You're cute. You know it?"

"We might be able to help each other out."

"That's what you said on the phone. But I haven't heard a goddamn thing yet."

"Show me yours and I'll show you mine," said Strange.

Vaughn chuckled. "For a nickel I will."

It was an old vulgar joke about a colored girl. Vaughn was indelicate. Vaughn's kind were about to be extinct. He was the type of man Strange's mother would charitably call "a product of his time." Strange knew that Vaughn was that way. He was also good police.

"What I got for you is real," said Strange. "That's a promise."

"Now you're gonna bargain."

"Why wouldn't I?"

"You always were smart. It's a damn shame you left the force."

"I had to," said Strange.

Vaughn tapped ash off his cigarette. "I like a guy named Robert Lee Jones for this one. Goes by Red."

"Red Jones."

"You heard of him?"

"Sure."

"Got a nice long rap sheet. Relatively small stuff up till now. Agg assaults and shit like that."

"You have a description?"

"Tall, light-skinned black. Reddish hair."

Strange took this in. "That would explain his street name."

"You'd think. Wears an Afro like you, but his is all fucked up. I've seen his latest mug shot. Looks like Stymie gone wrong."

"What's the motive?"

"Contract hit. Odum was one of my informants; he tipped me on a homicide I'd been working. The guy we arrested and charged probably arranged the murder-for-hire from inside the jail."

"I know Odum washed dishes up at Cobb's. What's that pay, dollar sixty-two an hour? You say he was your CI, but even with that, how did he afford that apartment and his heroin habit?"

"He was a tester, so the jolts were free. Could be he was living off his old B-Ones. Bobby always found a way to make it. Career criminal, but no violence." Vaughn dragged on his L&M and let the smoke out slow. "He was a good egg."

"How'd you come to all this knowledge?"

"Red Jones robbed and shot a small-time heroin dealer by the name of Roland Williams. Williams lived to finger Jones and describe an unidentified accomplice: a little man with gold teeth. Odum was a tester for Williams. Odum must have put Jones onto Williams before he got done. I think it connects."

"You think."

"Yeah."

"So pick up Jones."

"We would if we could find him. His photo's been passed out at roll call in every district. He's on parole, but his PO says he hasn't reported to her in months. The Absconding Unit's been looking for him, but so far they've come up with bupkes. His last known address is bullshit. My informants don't know anything, either, or they're too afraid to talk. If he's driving a car it's not registered."

"That's where I might be able to help you."

"Hold up a second." Vaughn stubbed out his cigarette and signaled the owner of the diner. "Hey, Nick, gimme a Hershey bar, will you? I need somethin sweet to go with this coffee."

"Male or female?" said Nick.

"With nuts," said Vaughn. As Nick went down to the register, where the candy was racked in a display, Vaughn returned his attention to Strange. "Go ahead."

"A source of mine saw a man, matches your description of Red Jones, on Thirteenth at the time of the murder. My source heard a small-caliber gunshot right before the man exited the Odum building."

"Will your source testify?"

"Hell, no," said Strange. "He won't talk to the law, on or off the record. And I'm not about to give him up."

"I'm still listening," said Vaughn. He unwrapped the Hershey bar Nick had dropped before him, broke off a piece, and popped it into his mouth.

"Jones, if it *was* Jones, got into a red late-model Plymouth, white interior."

"A Plymouth what?"

"Fury, had fold-in headlamps."

"That would make it a seventy-one." Vaughn nodded, thinking of Martina Lewis, seated beside him in the auditorium of the Lincoln Theatre. *I heard him called Red Fury, too. I don't know why.* "Sonofabitch."

"What?"

"I think my dick's gettin hard."

"Wait'll you hear the rest."

"Tell me."

"There was a woman driving the Fury. Tall, from what my source could make out. Had dark skin and big hair."

"Your source didn't happen to get the numbers on the plates?"

"No."

"Shit."

" 'Cause there weren't any numbers," said Strange with a small smile. "They were vanity plates."

"You don't say."

"Plates read 'Coco.' C-O, C-O."

Vaughn slid off his stool and stood. "D.C. tags, right?"

"Correct."

Vaughn put another cigarette in his mouth, lit it, and went to the house pay phone, where he made a call. Strange got up, walked down to the end of the counter, and got the attention of the grill woman, who said her name was Ida. Strange complimented her on her cooking, thanked her for her kindness in making his eggs southern, and slipped her a couple of dollar bills. He met Vaughn at the register, where he was hurriedly settling up with Nick.

"I got this," said Vaughn.

"Did you see me reach?" said Strange.

"Thanks, Marine," said Nick, closing the register drawer.

Vaughn and Strange walked toward their cars, parked together on Vermont.

"Your mom doing all right?" said Vaughn.

"She's fine," said Strange. "Working for an eye doctor downtown."

"I've been by the Three-Star. Heard your dad passed. My sympathies."

"Thank you."

Vaughn stopped walking, hit his cigarette, hot-boxed it with one last drag, and flicked the butt out to the street.

"If you happen to come up on that ring..." said Strange.

"Right," said Vaughn. "Watch yourself out there."

"I plan to."

They shook hands.

NINE

LOU FANELLA stood beside the bed of Roland Williams in D.C. General Hospital. Gino Gregorio leaned against a wall.

There had been a nurse taking Williams's vitals when they'd arrived, and Fanella had asked her to give them some privacy. He'd smiled at her in a way that implied no kindness and said, "Don't go telling anyone we're in here, sweetheart. I might take that to mean we're not friends." She left them with her eyes downcast and closed the door behind her. Outside the hospital, dusk had come, throwing long shadows on the stadium-armory complex grounds. A faint gray light had settled in the room.

"Who robbed you?" said Fanella, looking down at Williams. "Don't take too long thinking about it, either. I don't have the patience or the time."

"He goes by the name of Red," said Williams without hesitation. "Red Jones. Don't know what the minister called him when he got baptized."

"How'd you know it was him?"

"I knew him by rep. Tall, light-skinned dude with a fucked-up head of hair, kinda rusty like."

"Who hipped him to your supply?"

"Tester of mine name Bobby Odum. Jones deaded Odum, then he and this little dude with gold teeth came after me."

"And they ripped you off for your product."

"At the point of a gun," said Williams.

"Funny he didn't do you all the way."

"Wasn't for lack of tryin."

"It was me, I would have put one in your head."

"The man shot me," said Williams, seeing where Fanella was going and not liking it. "Close range, with a forty-five. You think I'd let him do me like that for *what?* To *pretend* I got robbed?"

Fanella looked down on Williams and stared him in the eyes. "It makes me wonder, is all."

"I'm a businessman. You can ask Jimmy, up at One Sixteenth. I'm straight." He was speaking on Jimmy Compton, Fanella and Gregorio's man in Harlem.

"Me and Gino already spoke to Jimmy," said Fanella. "Now we're speaking to you."

"Okay," said Williams. "All right." Bullets of sweat had risen on his forehead.

"Tell us where we can find the heroin," said Fanella. "Or the money. Makes no difference to me."

"Po-lice got half of the dope," said Williams. "I only told Red where *some* of it was. Tried to keep it from him, see? But the law found the rest of it, in the spot where I keep it."

"Where's that?"

"At my crib."

"So half of it's gone for good."

Williams thought to say something, but his mouth was dry. He felt his lip tremble. He tried to make it stop, but he could not.

Fanella smiled. "You all right?"

"Yes," said Williams. He was ashamed and he looked away.

"Let me see what Red did to you."

"Why?"

"I'm curious." Fanella looked over his shoulder and said, "Gino."

Gregorio moved to the door and put his back against it.

"Don't," said Williams.

"Don't?"

"Sayin, I wish you wouldn't do that. Doctor said to leave it be."

"C'mon," said Fanella, his thick eyebrows meeting comically as he mustered up a false face of concern. "Lemme see."

Fanella pulled his switchblade from the pocket of his sport jacket and opened it with the touch of a button. The blade locked into a place with a soft click. Williams recoiled and made a small humming sound. Fanella chuckled as he cut the sling from Williams's shoulder. Then he used the knife to slice away the bandages that covered his wound. Williams winced at the wet sucking sound of gauze pulling away from dressing and skin.

"Wow," said Fanella. "You should look at this, Gino."

Gregorio did not move.

"Please, man," said Williams.

"That's a big hole," said Fanella. The entrance wound was

the size of a quarter, black around the edges, pinkish in the center where the skin had begun to come back, slick and shiny from the dressing. "Don't even look like it's infected."

"Please."

"What'd you tell the police?"

"What I told *you*. I gave up Red's name. That's all."

"They found heroin in your apartment and they're not even going to charge you?"

"It was an *ex*change, 'cause I gave up good information. Plus, they searched my spot without a warrant."

"You said you knew Red's rep. So you must know more."

"I told the law enough to leave me alone."

"I'm not the law," said Fanella. "What'd you leave out?"

"I can't say no more, for real. I'm not tryin to get doomed."

Fanella put one knee up on the mattress to steady himself. He loosely placed his hand on Williams's shoulder above the wound and kept his thumb free.

"What didn't you tell them?" Fanella grinned. "What else?"

"Red got this woman," said Williams, a tremor in his voice. "Goes by Coco. Runs whores in a house on Fourteenth. What I heard, anyway."

"Heard where?"

"The street." Williams gave him the location and described the building.

"That's it?"

"Swear for God."

Fanella gripped Williams shoulder. "Does this hurt?"

"No."

"How about this?" Fanella pushed his thumb into the

gunshot wound. It felt like jelly as he broke through the skin. Williams began to thrash and scream.

"Lou," said Gregorio, and turned his head away.

Fanella put his right hand over the man's mouth. Williams urinated on the sheets before he passed out.

"Niggers aggravate me," said Fanella.

They left the room and walked down the hall. They did not move quickly, because Lou Fanella felt that a man should leave a scene unhurried, with his shoulders square and chin up. They went by a nurse who did not notice them, and an aged orderly pushing a wheelchair, and a tall, uniformed security guard with chiseled features who was standing against a wall, giving them a long stare.

"Fuck you lookin at?" said Fanella to the young man.

"Nothin, sir."

"I didn't think so."

Clarence Bowman studied them as they passed.

FRANK VAUGHN sat in an unmarked Dodge beside Detective Henry A. Passman, a gentle family man who, because of his initials, was called "Hap" by nearly everyone on the force. Like many career police officers who aspired to rise above uniform status, he had been shuttled around various divisions and had finally found a home in what had once been Prostitutions and Perversions but was now known by the more succinct description of Vice.

Night had come to the city. The calendar said close to summer, and there were folks dressed lightly and out on the street. On 14th at R, a spring-gold '70 Camaro, up on HiJackers, was curbside, idling. A white girl in white hot pants and a red gingham midriff shirt was leaning into its open driver's-side window, negotiating with the muscle car's occupants. Music was coming loudly from the eight-track system, but to Vaughn it was just screams and guitars. His focus was on the girl, a minor from the looks of her, and the heads of the five long-haired young men squeezed into the car.

"It's somebody's birthday," said Vaughn.

"One of the boys in the backseat just turned sixteen," said Passman. "His pals are buying him a present."

"The Fourteenth Street cherry-bust. A rite of passage in this town."

"They don't want a white girl, though. They can get that any day at their high school. This one's gonna take the money and turn the boy over to one of the black girls in the stable."

"Then?"

"The boy's directed to a building and told to go up a flight of stairs. Imagine what that's like. How his heart's pounding. Boy's never even been down here before and now he's in a strange house in what he thinks of as the ghetto. So he meets his whore in a dark little room. She tells him straight away he has to use a rubber. Offers to put it on for him, and if he says no, she insists. She doesn't want to get on her back, is what it is. More often than not, that boy's gonna shoot while she's fittin the safe on his pecker."

"Liftoff," said Vaughn. "Bit of a letdown, isn't it?"

"He'll be *grateful*. Matter of fact, he'll go back to his friends with a spring in his step. Bragging about how he fucked a black chick."

"You got a daughter, Hap?"

"Two. I keep 'em close."

"My son's twenty-six and he still lives in my house, rent free. Olga stocks his bathroom with toilet paper, Hai Karate, and his favorite brand of minty toothpaste."

"Least you know where he is."

A signal came from the handheld radio on the seat by Passman's side. It was a plainclothes officer who had been sent into the Coco Watkins house and was now up in a room with one of the girls. He was telling Passman that the transaction had been made and that his girl had been badged. Passman switched frequencies and radioed a couple of squad cars that were parked on nearby side streets, waiting for his call. They arrived, sirens and cherry-tops activated, shortly thereafter, accompanied by a wagon. The Camaro promptly sped off, and the white girl disappeared into an alley.

"Life's off-key symphony," said Passman, a cut-rate philosopher toiling in a world of hookers, pimps, glory-hole enthusiasts, flagellants, women who spread their legs on the D.C. Transit, and guys who played with their dongs in public.

"Let's see what we got inside," said Vaughn.

The building had been a row house, once residential, now zoned commercial, with an urban market on the first floor. They followed the uniformed police into the door beside the market and went up a flight of stairs to the second floor. The uniforms had drawn their service revolvers, but Vaughn's rig remained snapped. At the sound of the sirens, Red Jones would have gone out the fire escape that led to the alley, where another patrolman and his partner were stationed and ready. But those officers had radioed in that all was quiet. Vaughn had not expected to find Jones in the building. He was here for information.

The undercover officer and the unlucky young whore were standing in the hall, his hand loosely gripping her upper arm. She was an unformed-looking girl in a purple negligee. A prominent mole marked her face. Two other girls were standing in the hall, similarly attired, observing, smoking cigarettes.

"Entrapment," said the girl, whose name was Shay. "Entrapment." She had been told to repeat that word and nothing else.

"Down at the end," said the plainclothes man to Passman and Vaughn.

They didn't need to be told. Coco Watkins, in red lipstick, violet eye shadow, high heels, high hair, and a red dress, stood by an open door at the end of hot-pad row, leaning against the frame. Her arms were folded. Her breasts were like chocolate grapefruits heaving up out of her plunging V-neck.

"All right, that's enough," said Vaughn, and the uniformed police holstered their guns.

As Vaughn approached Coco, he noted that he was looking her straight in the eye. Wasn't often that he came upon a woman his height. Her evening shoes gave her three inches, but even without them, she had to be six foot tall.

Passman showed her his badge.

"Question is," said Coco, "who is he?"

"Detective Frank Vaughn," he said, dipping his head cordially.

"Hound Dog," said Coco, one corner of her lip upturned in a half smile. "Y'all got a warrant?"

"Why don't you just be polite and ask us in," said Passman.

"Don't touch anything," said Coco. "I'm not playin."

She unfolded her arms and walked into her apartment, which was also her office. Vaughn and Passman followed. To Vaughn it looked like the lair of a proper madam. Red velvet sofa, a nice big bed, and a bar cart, fully stocked.

"Drink?" said Coco, reading Vaughn's eyes.

Vaughn shook his head.

"We're placing your girl under arrest for solicitation," said Passman. "You, too, and the others."

"This here is a licensed massage establishment."

"You'll get a phone call," said Passman.

"*Shit.*" She looked at Vaughn. "I know why Vice made my door dark. Why you here?"

"I'm looking for Robert Lee Jones," said Vaughn. "Goes by Red."

"So?"

"He's wanted on suspicion of a homicide. You and Red are friends, aren't you?"

"Maybe we are. But I don't know where he is at this time. If you run into him—"

"I know. Give him your regards." Vaughn looked around, saw a closed door. "Is that a closet?"

"Go ahead and look in it. While you're at it, search under the bed, you got a mind to."

Vaughn's eyes were drawn to the bed. It was a brass-rail deal, the box spring and mattress up high. He could see the edge of a wooden box beneath it, sitting on the floor. Many straights kept their valuables close by, underneath their beds. Criminals did, too. Vaughn glanced at Coco's manicured hands, unadorned with jewelry.

"I doubt Red Jones is hiding under anyone's bed," said Vaughn.

"Believe it, big man."

Coco looked at Vaughn directly. Vaughn smiled.

"I don't need no bracelets, Hap," said Coco.

"Right," said Passman, turning to one of the cops in uniform. "Take her out. Gently."

Out in the hall, as the girls were being led to the stairs, Coco watched Shay, her head down, her hair disheveled, being moved along by the undercover man. Shay was one of the newer ladies, and this was her first arrest. It would not be the only emotional hit she'd take that night.

Coco felt bad for Shay, almost. But it was time for her to see this life as it was instead of how she wanted it to be. Girl had to learn.

Vaughn was the last one out of the building. He checked the front door before stepping onto the street.

TEN

AT **HALF** past ten that night, a bloody and beaten man named Dallas Butler walked into the Third District police station at 16th and V, Northwest, went directly to the desk sergeant, and said, "I wanna confess to the murder of Robert Odum. I'm turning myself in."

Sergeant Bill Herbst, black-haired and beefy, pointed to a row of chairs. "Have a seat over there and wait."

A few minutes later, Vaughn came out from the offices and found Butler, a uniformed cop now standing beside him. Vaughn studied Butler, a young man with wide shoulders and thick hands. His lower lip was split as if filleted, and one eye was swollen shut. There was a raised welt on his left cheek, and the ear on the same side was as big and misshapen as a gourd.

Blood was splattered all over the front of his white shirt, and blood had crusted beneath his mouth.

"You are?"

"Dallas Butler."

"I understand you want to talk about a homicide."

"Yes, sir."

"It's Detective Vaughn." He put out his hand. Butler gripped it weakly. "C'mon back and get cleaned up."

Vaughn helped Butler up and guided him back into the main offices, which were not traditional offices but rather an open room of desks. Across the room, Coco Watkins, Shay, and the rest of the girls were finalizing their processing by Passman and a couple of the junior members of his squad. Coco's lawyer, Jake Tempchin, who serviced many in the D.C. underworld, had arrived and was talking loudly and gesturing broadly at Passman and other police, who were going about their paperwork and pointedly not looking at him.

"Dallas!" said Shay when she noticed her man crossing the room. Her hand went to her mouth, an involuntary shock response at seeing Butler in his woeful condition.

"Shut up, girl," said Coco.

Butler glanced over at his lady friend, made no acknowledgment, then lowered his head and kept walking. But Vaughn had caught the connection.

Butler was put into one of the interview rooms, which held a scarred table-and-chairs arrangement. Beside one chair a leg iron had been bolted to the floor, and on the table were an ashtray, a tape recorder, and a yellow legal pad. Vaughn sent in Officer Anne Honn, blond and womanly, who was the unofficial station house nurse and the object of much attention from her male coworkers. She commenced to working on Butler with alcohol swabs and antiseptics. Honn told Vaughn that Butler needed to go to a hospital, that at the very least his lip was going to need stitches. Vaughn agreed with her assessment, adding that it would have to wait. He turned to Butler.

"Your name is really Dallas?"

"Says Leonard on my birth certificate."

"I'll be back in a few," said Vaughn. "You need water?"

"I'd rather have a soda."

"Okay." Vaughn lifted his deck of cigarettes from his inside pocket and dropped them on the table, along with a pack of matches. He never left his lighter in these rooms.

Butler eyed Vaughn's L&Ms with disappointment. "Can I get a menthol?"

"I'll give it a try."

Vaughn exited the room. He got Passman's attention, took him aside, and learned that Coco and the others would spend the night in jail, then be arraigned, bailed by Tempchin via a bondsman, and bounced the following day. In all probability the laborious and useless process would end in a fine. Passman asked Shay if she would speak with Detective Vaughn, but she refused.

Vaughn returned to his desk. He ran Butler's name through the card system and made some phone calls, the first to the Absconding Unit, the last to Lorton Reformatory. All of that took an hour. On the way back to the interview room he bought a Nehi from a machine and hit up a young black detective, Charles Davis, for a couple of Newports.

He went back into the room, sat across the table from Butler, put down the orange soda, and rolled two Newports in his direction. Butler picked one up and fitted it carefully into the corner of his mouth. Vaughn readied an L&M, produced his lighter, put fire to Butler's cigarette, and fired up his own. He let the nicotine hit his lungs and exhaled a long stream of satisfaction over the table. Butler closed his eyes dreamily as he dragged on his smoke.

Vaughn simultaneously pressed two buttons, play and record, on the machine, and stated the date and time.

"Let's begin."

"I'm ready."

"Dallas is an unusual street name."

"It's my nickname. My mother's been a Cowboys fan since nineteen sixty. I'm the same way."

"You from here?"

"Straight D.C."

"But you don't root for the Redskins."

"Hail to Old *Dixie?* Please. I *can't* root for 'em."

There were many black residents of the Washington area who supported the Cowboys. The Redskins, under previous owner George Preston Marshall, were the last team to integrate in the NFL. Some locals would never forget.

"You're the Leonard Butler who busted out of Lorton on April nineteenth, correct?"

"Uh-huh."

"Lotta people been looking for you, Dallas."

"Here I am."

"And now you want to confess to the murder of Bobby Odum."

"Robert Odum, yes, sir."

"Why?"

"On account of I killed him."

"What was your motive?"

"I just didn't like the man."

"Must have been a strong *dis*like."

"It was."

"Where'd he live again?"

Butler gave Vaughn the correct address of Odum's building and added, "Second floor."

"How'd you get the better of him? I mean, you got some size on you, Dallas. But Odum had to be what, six-three or -four?"

"Bobby? You could put him in your pocket."

"Wasn't too sporting of you to shoot him in the back."

"It was the back of the *head*. Twice."

"Thirty-Eight, right?"

"Twenty-Two, Colt Woodsman."

"That particular gun makes you a contract man."

"If the shoe fits," said Butler, "you got to put it on."

"I don't think so," said Vaughn.

They stopped speaking for a while and enjoyed their cigarettes. The smoke hung thick in the small space. It irritated their eyes and nose hairs, but they smoked on. Butler dragged deeply on his Newport and added to the cloud in the room.

"Back to Odum..." said Vaughn.

"Right."

"I'm on the old side, case you haven't noticed," said Vaughn. "Been at this a long while. Can't even tell you how many times I've sat in rooms like this one, talking to murderers. Some of them acted on impulse, or out of rage or jealousy. Some of them planned their deed well in advance. Different reasons and motives, but they all had one thing in common. They had the capacity to pull the trigger or twist the knife. What I mean is, they could kill. You? You don't have that thing in you, young man."

"No?"

"There's nothing in your sheet to suggest it. No violence. Even the crime that got you your sixteen. Armed robbery? Shit, you weren't even armed. Your *accomplice* had the gun."

"You get inside those walls, you learn."

"It's not in your eyes." Vaughn hit his cigarette one last time and crushed the cherry. "That day you robbed the market. What were you up on, some kinda dope?"

Butler shook his head and spoke softly. "Swiss Colony wine."

"Took a couple a fifths of Bali Hai to jack up your courage, didn't it, Dallas? *Didn't* it?"

Butler looked away.

"You didn't kill anyone," said Vaughn.

"Wanna speak to an attorney."

"I already know that Red Jones murdered Odum. Who beat your ass and sent you in here to confess? Was it Jones?"

Butler crossed his arms. His cigarette had burned down to the filter. "Send me back to Lorton. I don't even *like* it out here no more."

"First you need to tell me who did this to you."

"I can't, man."

"Why not?"

"My mother."

Vaughn leaned forward. "Tell me about it."

"They threatened to do my mom if I didn't turn myself in."

"Jones?"

"And his partner."

"Little man with gold teeth."

"Alfonzo Jefferson."

Vaughn pulled a pen from his jacket and wrote the name

down on a pad. "Does your mother have someone she can live with until we can get these guys off the street?"

Butler nodded. "My sister stays over in Maryland with her husband and kids."

"I'll send someone to your mom's place. We'll tell her to move to your sister's for a while."

"My brother-in-law's not gonna like that," said Butler. But he gave Vaughn his mother's address.

"They worked you over pretty good," said Vaughn.

"It was mostly Fonzo."

"Why'd he have to do you like that?"

"*Had to* got nothin to do with it." Butler lit his second cigarette off the one still burning.

"Where can I find those two?"

"I don't know. I was supposed to meet with, you know, this girl I see. I went to the spot, and they rolled up on me instead. Took me into an alley."

"Rolled up in what?"

"Gold deuce-and-a-quarter with skirts. Nice-lookin car... a sixty-eight."

"Hard or soft top?"

"Hard."

Vaughn wrote this down. "The girl is the one out in the office with the mole on her face. That's how you got involved in all this?"

"Shay," said Butler. "Nice little gal."

"She looks it."

"Don't be rough on her, man. She didn't know. Red told me so hisself."

"I'm not looking to add to her problems."

"She ain't had no problem with me."

"No?"

"I hit that thing right." Butler smiled reflectively. "She got some good pussy on her, man."

"It's all good when it's young." Vaughn got up out of his chair. "You need some medical attention before they put you back. I'll just get that going for you. Get you some more cigarettes, too."

"Y'all talk to my mother," said Butler, "please don't tell her I got beat. I don't want the old girl to worry."

"Not a problem."

Vaughn left the room and closed the door behind him. Passman was still working, but Coco, the ladies, and their lawyer were gone. Vaughn gave some instructions to Officer Anne Honn regarding Butler's treatment and his mother. He then went to his desk, had a seat, picked up his phone, and got Derek Strange at his apartment. He told Strange what he'd seen in Coco's bedroom, and the window of opportunity that existed, most likely, for just one night. He described the layout of the building and its front door.

Vaughn then phoned Olga. He told her he loved her. He told her he had paperwork to do and not to wait up.

Out in the lot, he got into his Monaco and headed uptown. Vaughn stopped at the Woodnar on 16th Street, past the lion bridge, and went up to Linda Allen's apartment.

"How about a drink for an old friend?" said Vaughn when Linda opened her door.

She put a June Christy record on the console stereo and fixed a couple of cocktails. They had some laughs and fucked like animals in her bed.

ELEVEN

ALFONZO JEFFERSON had a spot in the high fifties, in a place known as Burrville in far Northeast, the populous but least-mentioned quadrant of the city, forgotten by many in power, mysterious and virtually unknown to most suburban commuters. Jefferson rented a two-story asbestos-shingled house near Watts Branch Park, on a sparsely built block whose houses sat on large pieces of land. It was an urban location with a country vibe. A few kept chickens in their backyards, and one old man had a goat on a chain. It was quiet here, and that suited Jefferson fine.

Jefferson had no checkbook or Central Charge card. He paid a man cash to live in the house. The rent was a little bit more than the surroundings warranted, but the extra was for utilities and such. Jefferson didn't want his name on any bills. As for his car, he had bought it from the Auto Market at 3rd and Florida and had this girl, Monique Lattimer, put her name on the title and registration. Come tax time, Jefferson wrote "handyman" in the space they had for occupation. He claimed he earned little income and paid nothing or sometimes pennies to the government. He used his mother's address when he had to, and it was an old address. He was as invisible as a man could be.

He was seated in the living room, which held worn, heavily cushioned furniture grouped around a cable spool table. Jefferson, wearing a woven brimmed hat indoors, looked small in the big high-back chair. Red Jones and Clarence Bowman were on the couch. They were drinking Miller High Lifes out of bottles and huffing cigarettes. Monique Lattimer was somewhere in the house, but Jefferson had asked her to leave the room. They could hear her moving around up on the second floor.

"Tempchin say Coco and the girls gonna be out tomorrow," said Jones. "She got word to me through the lawyer. Said it was that detective, Vaughn, was in on the bust. He's lookin for me on the Odum thing."

"Thought you left outta there clean," said Jefferson.

"I did," said Jones. "The loose piece was Roland Williams. Ain't that right, Clarence?"

Bowman, who wore a security guard uniform during the day, was now smart in street clothes from the Cavalier Men's Shop. He was the quiet type and had spoken little since arriving at Jefferson's house. "Vaughn and that half-man prosecutor paid him a visit."

"Cochnar," said Jones.

"They weren't the only ones," said Bowman. "Two other white boys came by, looked like professionals. When they left, the nurses came runnin and shit, 'cause those white boys had laid some kind of hurtin on Williams."

"That means Williams talked to them, too," said Jones. "I shoulda killed that motherfucker dead."

"What'd the white boys look like?" said Jones.

"Spaghetti benders," said Bowman. "One dark, one blond."

Bowman didn't say much unless it was important, but he had a way with a phrase and an offbeat sense of humor. Used to do these funny imitations of neighborhood folks when he and Jones were kids, back when they were just starting out, learning from the older hustlers in the original Temperance Court. That was before the government moved their families to another location. Some still called the old alley dwelling Square 274, with bitterness and fondness, both at once, in their tone.

"They lookin for the heroin we took," said Jones. "Must be from up north."

"What's that got to do with me?" said Bowman.

"Nothin," said Jones.

"Then say why you brought me here," said Bowman. "I got a freak waitin on me in the car."

"Want you to do your thing," said Jones. He crushed out a smoked-down Kool in an ashtray.

"Roland Williams?"

"I'll take care of him my *own* self."

"Who, then?"

"The prosecutor."

"Cochnar?" said Bowman. "That's some high-profile shit."

"You'll be paid."

"I'm gonna have to be *well* paid."

"Ain't no thing. Me and Fonzo are flush, and we about to get richer."

"I know you're good." Bowman abruptly got up, smoothed the front of his triple-pleated slacks, and put out his hand. "Two Seventy-Four."

"Two Seven Four," said Jones, giving his old friend a thumb-grip shake, moving their hands from side to side.

Bowman nodded at Jefferson and left the house.

"Your boy look like Rafer Johnson," said Jefferson.

"Clarence's face cut the same way," said Jones.

Jefferson got up and put an album on the platter of his compact system. It was the new Kool and the Gang, *Music Is the Message*. He dropped the needle on the song called "Soul Vibrations." As it came forward he said, "This jam is *bad* right here."

Jones made no comment. He didn't care much for music or books. He liked movies when he had the time, the ones had black men in charge, but mostly his focus was on work. He aimed to leave behind a name that would be remembered. That would be something. Maybe the only thing. The one way you could win. 'Cause everyone was bound for a bed of maggots in the end.

"I could use another blonde," said Jones.

Jefferson called out to his woman, and soon Monique appeared in the room. She was taller than Jefferson. The tops of her globes came bold out of her shirt, and she had straightened hair that was left uncombed. Monique had a mean-mustang look to her that Jones liked. He wondered what it would take to make an untamed country girl like her smile.

"Get us two more High Lifes, Nique," said Jefferson.

Monique flattened a palm on her hip. "Your legs broke?"

Jefferson smiled a row of gold. "Shake a tail feather, baby."

Monique turned on one heel and went to the fridge to get their beer.

"Lotta woman right there," said Jones.

"That girl can buck."

After she returned with their beverages and left the room again, they discussed their plans. There was much to do.

STRANGE PULLED his Monte Carlo over to the curb on 14th a block north of the house where Coco Watkins plied her trade. It was now well past two in the morning. Last call had come and gone. The licensed bars had closed their doors, and though there were many after-hours establishments down here, bottle clubs, floating card games, and such, most were in side street row homes, not on the main avenue. There were folks here and there, some standing on corners, a couple of them staggering and plain wasted. Others walked toward their homes, minding their own. But the general landscape was quiet. Even the punchboards had called it a night.

Strange walked down the sidewalk unarmed. He had a retractable baton in the trunk of his car and sometimes he carried a Buck knife. But he was about to commit a B-1, and to have a weapon attached to it meant mandatory time. His aim was to get in, find what he was looking for, and get out. No violence, no complications.

As he approached the door beside the market, he quickly scanned the area and saw no one who appeared to be law. He was unconcerned with witnesses. His plan was to enter the house as if he owned it. He put his hand inside his sleeve, turned the knob on the open door, stepped inside, and closed the door behind him.

He stood silently in a kind of small foyer and listened. He heard nothing but the ticks and creaks an old house made in the middle of the night. He reached into the back pocket of his jeans and produced a pair of latex gloves that he'd taken from a box Carmen had brought home from the hospital. He fitted the gloves on his hands.

"Hey!" said Strange, and heard only the echo of his own voice.

He went up the stairs, his gloved right hand riding the banister up to the second-floor landing. He knew where he was going because Vaughn had detailed the layout. But first he needed to ensure an alternate exit. Instead of heading straight to Coco's office, he went in the opposite direction, down a hall, past a row of small rooms that ended with a dirty window leading out to a fire escape going down to the alley.

Strange unlatched the window. As he did it, he heard a noise from the first floor. A knock on the door, and then the door swinging open. Two men, talking loudly and unconcerned about the racket they were making. Then their footsteps, heavy on the stairs.

FANELLA AND Gregorio ascended the staircase. Gregorio had a .38 holstered inside his jacket. Beneath Fanella's white raincoat was an Ithaca pump-action twelve-gauge that had been cut down and fitted in a sling. Gregorio pulled his revolver as his feet hit the landing and waited for Fanella's instructions. Fanella looked toward the front of the building, saw an open door that led to a large room. He moved his chin in that direction, and Gino Gregorio pointed the gun there. It was understood that he would shoot if he felt the need.

Fanella opened his raincoat and drew the shotgun. He proceeded to walk down the hall methodically, looking carefully into each open room, kicking in the doors of those that were closed. It was soon obvious to him that these rooms were empty. Still, they approached the main room gun-ready. Only when they stepped inside and saw that it was unoccupied did they lower their weapons.

They had seen the light in the window from the street. Fanella found it odd that there was no one here. He was confounded, and he was somewhat disappointed. He looked around at the red furniture, the red velvet drapes, the brass bed.

"Least we come to the right place, Gino."

"It's a whorehouse, Lou."

"You think?"

Fanella slipped the shotgun into the sling, then walked to a bar cart and picked up a bottle of Crown Royal. He poured some into a tumbler, drank half of it down, made a sour face, and dropped the glass to the floor.

"What's wrong?"

"Some boofer poured rotgut into a Royal bottle."

They tossed the room but found no heroin. Before they exited, Gregorio watched Fanella reach into a box and drop something in his pocket.

"Who's that for?" said Gregorio.

Fanella said, "My wife."

*　　*　　*

WHEN STRANGE was certain they had left, he reentered the house. He'd watched them, sitting as far back as possible on the fire escape, through the dirty window. He'd made out their race, size, hair color, guns, and the white raincoat the larger man wore.

Strange went down the hall to the large office, where a light had been left on. Carefully, he moved the curtain slightly aside on one of the big windows fronting 14th and looked down at the street. A large dark-haired man and a lean one with blondish hair were getting into a late-'60s black Lincoln. From this vantage point, the origin and numbers on the plates were unreadable. The car started with deep ignition and pulled away from the curb.

Strange had a quick look around. The men had turned the place over indelicately and searched the room thoroughly. A big wooden box, the kind used to hold silverware, sat on the floor beside the bed.

It was the box described by Vaughn. It had been opened and remained open still. There were only a few trinkets left inside. Necklaces of colored glass, a tiara with broken rhinestones, and a cameo brooch that looked to be made of plastic. All kinds of cheap, imitation jewelry.

Strange moved his hand through the goods. He found no ring.

TWELVE

FRANK VAUGHN pushed his plate aside, picked up his deck of L&Ms, and shook out a smoke. He lit the cigarette with his Zippo, placed the lighter atop the pack, and pulled an ashtray within reach. Before him was a notepad and pen.

"I'll have some more java, Nick."

"Sure thing, Marine." Nick Michael, owner and operator of the Vermont Avenue diner, took Vaughn's empty and moved to the big urns, where he drew a cup of fresh coffee. He returned to the counter with the full cup and placed it in Vaughn's saucer. To the young black man with the thick mustache and broad shoulders, seated beside Vaughn, Nick said, "How 'bout you, young fella, want me to warm that up?"

"I'm good," said Strange. He had already devoured his eggs, scrapple, and onions fried in hash browns, and sopped up the yolk with toast. Nick removed both of their plates and walked toward a bus pan down by the register.

"You get in that building all right?" said Vaughn.

"Thanks to you."

"Wish I'd stuck around."

"I was lookin through a dirty window, mostly, so I didn't have the best view."

"And you saw…"

"Two white men. One dark and on the big side, one thin and fair skinned. The big guy carried a shotgun. The other one had some kind of pistol."

"What about their vehicle?"

"Black late-sixties Lincoln with suicides."

Vaughn wrote that down on his pad. "Sounds like a match. Two white men visited Roland Williams and tortured him in D.C. General yesterday. A nurse gave us a rough description that's close to yours."

"Tortured him for what?"

"Williams says he doesn't recollect. I'm guessing they were after information on the whereabouts of Red Jones. If I'm right, Williams gave up the location of Coco Watkins's whorehouse. That's what they were doing there—looking for Red."

"Who are they?"

"Button men from up north," said Vaughn. "Italians. Williams copped heroin on consignment from a guy up in Harlem who was connected to the Organization. So Roland Williams, in effect, owed money to the Mob. Jones took off Roland's stash. Now the Italians are looking for Jones to settle the debt."

"You know this?"

"Williams told me just enough to put it together. It makes sense."

"Red Jones is leaving behind a trail of fire."

"He's bold," said Vaughn. "Him and his partner, little dude named Alfonzo Jefferson, compelled a Lorton escapee, Dallas Butler, to come into the station last night and make a false confession to the murder of Bobby Odum."

"Compelled him how?"

"They beat the shit out of him and threatened to murder his mother. Butler's on the way back to jail, and happy to catch the ride. I did get one bit of information before I shipped him off."

"What's that?"

"Jefferson drives a sixty-eight Electra, gold exterior, hard-top with fender skirts."

"Deuce-and-a-quarter?"

"Uh-huh. Case you see it on the street…"

"I know. Proceed with caution."

"I'm guessing Jones is cribbed up with Jefferson some-where," said Vaughn. "Coco's trick pad is way too hot."

Strange borrowed a pen from Vaughn and wrote down the description of Jefferson's car on a napkin. He folded the napkin and slipped it in the pocket of his slacks.

"You happen to find Red," said Vaughn, "I wouldn't try to talk to him about any missing jewelry."

"Someone's gotta end this cat sooner or later."

"It's coming," said Vaughn. "Jones has a big set of nuts and he gives a good fuck about exactly nothin. But he's gonna bite it. Guys like him think they're taller than they are. They step on the wrong toes, and then it's assassination time. Darkness."

"Maybe you'll find him first."

"I hope I do," said Vaughn. He hit his cigarette and

studied it as he exhaled smoke. "I think I'm startin to love this guy."

"What's next?"

"I ran Alfonzo Jefferson through the system. He's got priors but he's no longer under supervision. Father deceased, no siblings on record. If his mother's alive, there's no record of her whereabouts. Prob'ly has a different last name than he does."

"Find the Electra, you find Jefferson."

"Right. There's a few Buicks in the city that match the description, but none under his name. I'll go out on the registration list and see if someone's carrying the paper for him. Talk to my informants, like that. You?"

"I'm thinking about taking a closer look at my client."

"Maybelline Walker? I don't blame you."

"I'm curious, is all."

"That broad's got a bag of cats under her dress. I met her, remember?"

"It's not like that," said Strange.

"Yeah, I know. You *like* her." Vaughn's grin was canine. "Deep down inside."

"Sayin, I'm spoken for. Got a date tonight with my girl, matter of fact. We're going to a show at Carter Barron."

"I took Olga there to see Henry Mancini and Harry Belafonte a few years ago. Mancini played 'Moon River,' and I acted like I cared."

Nick laid down the check between them, and Strange reached for his wallet. "I got this one."

"Stay in touch, Derek."

"I will."

Vaughn crushed out his L&M. Strange palmed a couple of dollars over the counter to the grill woman and settled up with Nick.

RED JONES and Alfonzo Jefferson sat in the gold Electra, parked nose east on Oglethorpe Street, in a neighborhood called Hampshire Knolls in Northeast. Their clothing was brightly colored, their heels were high, and the collars of their shirts were laid out wide across their chests. Jones had his .45 on the seat, resting against his leg. Jefferson's police-issue .38 was fit snugly between his legs.

Small homes, attached to one another in pairs, lined the block. The houses, built in 1950 and sold under the GI Bill, had originally gone for $12,000, with a mere $500 down payment the ticket in. Nearly all of those veterans and their young families were gone now, having moved out to suburban Maryland in search of better schools, safer streets, and whiter neighborhoods.

Mid-street, under the shade of a government oak, a boy buffed the milky film off a current-year Cadillac that he had washed and waxed. An older man sat in a folding chair in the same patch of shade, having a cigar while he watched the boy work.

"He up in that semidetached on the right," said Jefferson. "Ward visits the same woman, same day, every week about this time. Has that boy shine up his Caddy while he hits that thing."

"Kinda early for that, isn't it?"

"Man likes his morning glory."

"You do your homework, Fonzo."

"I try to."

"How long we got to sit here?"

"Boy's near finished. That means Ward about to come out."

Jones dragged on a cigarette, then let his smoking-hand rest on the lip of the open passenger-side window. "They say he buys a new short every year."

"Man's got to do somethin with all that cash."

"He spends plenty, but not all of it," said Jefferson, studying the Eldorado as if looking at it in a dream. "That's a sweet-ass car."

Sylvester Ward's latest had been purchased with cash. It was a triple-green coupe with an opera window, rear skirts, spoke wheels, and wide whitewalls. His vehicles were bought at Capitol Cadillac on 22nd Street in Northwest. He liked to say that he traded them in "when the ashtrays get full." If it was an exaggeration, it was not much of one.

Ward, a rotund man in his early forties, came out of the duplex. He walked with confidence and had the easy gait of a man who carried his weight naturally. He wore a forest-green suit with white stitching on the lapels, a textured white shirt, white shoes, and a white belt. The outfit was a deliberate complement to his car. Ward was dark, mostly, with small patches of beige on his cheeks and forehead, and spots of beige and white all over the backs of his hands. He had been afflicted with a skin condition since childhood.

"I see why they call him Two-Tone," said Jones.

"Look more like three to me," said Jefferson.

"Let's take him."

They gathered their guns, slipped them under the tails of their shirts, got out of the Electra, and commenced to cross the street. Jones paused to crush his cigarette under one of his Flagg Brothers, then deep-dipped forward.

Ward took note of the low-rent strangers as he descended the concrete steps of the row home. He showed no fear if he felt it, and when he hit the sidewalk he continued on toward his Cadillac. There they all met, standing around the car in that tight atmosphere that said some kind of conflict was about to go down. The boy dropped the chamois cloth he held in his hand and took one step back. The older man gripped the arms of the folding chair and stared straight ahead.

"What you two want?" said Ward tiredly.

Jones lifted his shirttail and showed Ward the butt of his .45. The boy's eyes widened and he felt his heart beat pleasantly in his chest. Nothing this exciting had ever happened to him and nothing would again. When he was a crushed and disappointed middle-aged man he would often bore his friends with the story of Red Jones, tall and proud, tight bells, tall stacks, big old Afro, who came up on him and his uncle, showed his heater, and took off numbers kingpin Sylvester Ward.

"You comin with us," said Jones. "Right now."

"Don't you know who I am?" said Ward, his voice a husky match to his size.

"Matter of fact, we do." Jefferson gave him a gold-toothed smile. "We ain't about to take no poor motherfucker off the street."

"Let's go," said Jones.

Ward gestured to the vehicle with incredulity. "What about my ride?"

"Leave it," said Jefferson. "The boy can watch it."

"Pay him for his time before you go," said Jones. He gave the boy a short nod.

Ward peeled off some bills from a roll of cash he drew from his pants pocket before walking with Jones and Jefferson to the Electra. Jones got into the backseat with Ward, drew his gun, and held it loosely in his lap.

Jefferson settled in behind the wheel of his car and turned the ignition. Looking in the rearview mirror at Ward, he said, "You stay over in Shepherd Park, right?"

"Holly Street," said Ward, just above a mumble.

Jefferson pulled away from the curb. "That's a nice El D, Two-Tone. What you got in that, a six?"

"*Shit*," said Ward. "That's a five-hundred-cubic-inch big-block V-eight."

"What do they call that color, ice-green, somethin?"

"*Willow*-green. It's new for this year."

"Pretty," said Jefferson.

That cut the conversation to nothing for a while. Jones drove south on New Hampshire, where he turned right onto Missouri Avenue and headed across town.

"Y'all kidnapping me," said Ward, as if it had just come to mind. "You know that's a capital crime."

"So?" said Jones.

"I got rid of my wife, and my kids are full grown and gone. They got nary a nickel from me, case you tryin to hold me for ransom..."

"We don't have the time for that," said Jones. "And you ain't all that important."

Little more was said for the rest of the ride. Ward sat

looking out the window, his hands in his ample lap, his lower lip thrust out like a hurt child's. Sylvester Ward was not frightened, but a piece had been chipped off his pride.

WARD LIVED on one of the tree-and-flower-named streets of Shepherd Park, the northernmost neighborhood before the Maryland line, west of Georgia and east of 16th Street. Most recently, its residents had actively resisted blockbuster realtors who had preyed on the fears of whites in post-riot D.C. Here, middle- and upper-middle-class blacks and whites lived side by side, and sometimes they lived under the same roof. It was one of the few uptown, upscale areas friendly to interracial couples. At one time, Jews who owned nearby Georgia Avenue businesses couldn't live in Shepherd Park. But that restriction, too, had been buried long ago with the other rotted corpses of the past.

When it came to women, Ward was tolerant running to liberal. He kept company with all kinds, but he was no political activist. He simply liked this area, with its brick and shingled single-family homes, large yards, shade trees, and flowery shrubs. He had paid cash for his house, as he did for everything he owned. He could have easily afforded a residence on the Black Gold Coast, down on North Portal Drive, with the professional, educated types, but he preferred to stay in Shepherd, which was nice but more down-home. He felt it was wise to remember where you came from and not pretend to be something you were not. The high branches of the tree die when the roots get cut. Like that.

Ward had been one of the city's top numbers men for some time. He didn't deal in ponies or the sports book. He had no knowledge of or interest in the drug or prostitution trades. He had come up in the policy game, where three-digit tickets could be bought for pocket change. He had runners all over the city; his employees were government messengers, dishwashers, janitors, and, in the old days, elevator operators. They were black men and they sold to all colors. They worked for a cut and were often tipped heavily by sentimental and superstitious winners. Above the runners were several men who kept the books and collected. The daily take, after the winning combination was paid out, was divided from small denominations and coin between Ward, his employees, and the New York Syndicate via a man in Baltimore whose nickname suggested royalty. It was claimed that there was no organized crime to speak of in D.C., and this was true in a sense, if one meant Mafia and Italian. But the Mob had long had their hands in the pockets of Washington's criminal element. The out-of-town payoff money was said to be well spent, as it kept the Syndicate at arm's length.

Ward's lottery business grossed millions of dollars a year. After the employees got paid, after New York got their cut, after Ward shelled out to locals of influence and power, he netted a hundred, a hundred and fifty grand annually. But he was good with that. His was an unexpectedly rewarding life. Ward was as cock-of-the-walk as it got for black Washington. He wasn't worried about jail or persecution. He was protected.

Which is why, walking into his house with his two abductors, Ward was more perplexed than angry. He wasn't used to being treated this way.

Ward removed his green jacket and draped it over the

back of an ornate dining-room chair. Jones, gun in hand, kept his eyes on Ward while Jefferson took in the opulence of his surroundings. Looked like a museum in here to him: crystal chandeliers, furniture with scrolled arms, oriental carpets, and plaster statues of naked white women and white men whose nuts hung lower than their dicks.

"I smell money," said Jefferson.

Ward shook his head slowly. "Obviously, y'all ain't done your due diligence."

"Huh?" said Jones.

"There ain't nothin here of value to speak of," said Ward. "Not the kind of payday you're looking for, anyway. Walkin-around money is all I got."

"We'll take what the fuck you *got*, then," said Jefferson.

"Get it," said Jones.

"It's up in my bedroom." But Ward did not move.

"You mean you ain't gone yet?" said Jones.

Jefferson drew his piece and pointed it to the stairs. Ward headed in that direction and Jefferson followed.

Jones went to a bar cart and chose a bottle of scotch that looked expensive. He poured amber liquor into a thick, etched tumbler and drank. Its velvet taste closed his eyes.

Jones had a second drink, and as he killed it, Ward and Jefferson returned to the living room. Jefferson had a fistful of cash in his free hand.

"Twenty-four hundred," said Jefferson. His tone was not exuberant.

"That's all?"

"I took his watch, too," said Jefferson. "Got diamonds around its face."

"That's cut glass," said Ward. "A bitch I know gave it to me as a present. I only wear it when she comes to visit."

"Gimme that watch on your arm, then," said Jones. "I know *that* ain't fake."

Ward laboriously removed a gold Rolex from his wrist. Jones slipped the timepiece onto his own wrist and examined it. It fit loose, the way he liked it.

"Now you done took everything I have," said Ward. Annoyance had come to his face.

Jones felt his pulse drum. "You got a roll in your pocket, too, fat man. Give it here."

Ward started to speak but bit down on his lip. He withdrew the cash, held together with a silver clip, and Jones slipped it into the patch pocket of his bells.

Jones looked Ward over. "Anyone ask you, it was Red Jones who took you for bad."

"Ain't nobody gonna ask," said Ward with naked contempt.

"Is that right."

"Ain't nobody care about you or what your name is," said Ward. "Ain't nobody gonna remember you when you're gone."

Jones' eyes were flat and he said nothing.

"You want my advice—"

"I don't," said Jones.

"Go on, then," said Ward, slashing his hand toward the front door of the house. "Get."

The barrel of the .45 was a blur as Jones's arm flared out. Its sight clipped Ward's nose and cut the bridge. Jones grunted as he put more into it and hit Ward squarely and violently in the same place again. Ward, too big to fall, staggered and gripped the arm of a chair for support. Blood flowed from his nostrils as it would have from an open spigot. Jones laughed and kicked the chair out from under him, and now Ward fell. He lay on his side on the hardwood floor, blood on his fine white shirt, one hand covering his nose, its cartilage smashed. Tears had sprung from his eyes and they were streaking down his face.

"Shouldn't have kept talkin," said Jones. "A man with *spots*, tryin to tell me what to do."

Red Jones and Alfonzo Jefferson left the house. They cut the cash up in the car.

THIRTEEN

MAYBELLINE WALKER lived in one of the apartment houses that lined 15th Street along the green of Meridian Hill, which many in the city now called Malcolm X Park. Drugged-out-looking whites, brothers and sisters with big naturals, and Spanish of indeterminate origin, some of the dudes wearing Carlos Santana–inspired headbands, streamed in and out of the park's entrances. A person could kick a soccer ball around, pay for a hand job or get one free, or score something for his head at Malcolm X, depending on the time of day. Its makeup had changed these past few years, but it remained one of the most beautiful open-to-the-public spots in the city. It wasn't but a short walk from Strange's crib; he often came over here when the sun was out to look at the talent and clear his mind.

Maybelline's Warwick-blue Firebird was parked on 15th. Strange had been in his Monte Carlo for a couple of hours now, since his breakfast with Vaughn, parked on the same street a block south. He was watching the folks come in and out the park, watching Maybelline's building, and listening to WOOK, the Isley Brothers covering "Love the One You're With," a hit for them on the soul charts, with cousin Chris Jasper's organ, the band's secret weapon, in the mix. Strange thinking, T-Neck, number 930. Just then, Maybelline emerged from the glass-front doors of her building and walked to her car.

"*Damn*," said Strange, an involuntary reaction, his mouth going dry at the sight of her, swinging her hips in a short strapless dress, the breeze blowing her hair away from her fine bare shoulders.

She dropped the ragtop of her Pontiac, ignitioned it, and drove north. Strange waited for a moment, then followed.

THERE WERE three owners whose cars fitted the description of a gold '68 Buick Electra registered in the District of Columbia. The first on the list, written neatly in his notebook, was a Dewight Mitchell. Mitchell's given address was on Adams Street in Bloomingdale, tucked in south of the McMillan Reservoir, just behind Howard U. Vaughn put his hat on, stepped out of his Monaco, and went up the steps to a brick house that held a steel-framed rocker sofa on its porch. There was no Electra on the street, but Vaughn knocked on the door anyway and did not get a response. From inside the house, a calico cat looked at him with boredom through a rectangular pane of glass.

Vaughn walked down to 2nd Street and cut into the alley that ran behind Adams. It was not a hunch but rather good procedure for D.C. investigators and uniformed police to check the alleyways when seeking interview subjects. For many Washingtonians, the alley served as the front yard.

He found a black woman, sturdy, with kind eyes, wearing slacks and a work shirt, resting on the shaft of a shovel by a plot of overturned dirt in the back of her property. He had counted the houses and knew that this was the Mitchell residence.

"Ma'am." Vaughn tipped his head and introduced himself over her chain-link fence. He flipped open his badge case and let her glance at his shield. "Are you Miss Mitchell?"

"Mrs.," said the woman. "I'm Henrietta, Dwight's wife." Several cats were in the yard, walking about but staying close to Henrietta. One with brown stripes on a gray coat was stretched out glamorously under her back steps. "What can I do for you?"

"Does your husband own a nineteen sixty-eight Buick Electra, gold with black interior?"

"That's our car," she said brightly. "My name's not on it, but it's mine, too. When he lets me drive it."

She was in her fifties, with graying, straightened hair that had a nice shine to it. From the way her bottom half filled out her slacks, he could see that she was young where it counted. Vaughn liked her manner and her looks.

"I didn't see the Buick out front."

"Dwight takes it to work."

"Where's his place of employment?"

She told him and asked, "What's this about?"

"I'm hoping to question the owner of a car like yours. But I'm pretty sure your husband isn't the man I'm looking for.

Does he ever loan out his vehicle? Let a friend drive it, something like that?"

"Not that I'm aware of. But you should ask him that yourself."

Henrietta looked down at the soil she had just turned over with the shovel. "I'm going to put in some tomato plants. Do you think I waited too long? It's awful late in the season, isn't it?"

"I wouldn't know," said Vaughn.

Vaughn hadn't pushed a lawnmower in twenty years and he'd never planted a garden in his life. He paid neighborhood kids to take care of his yard. He had no hobbies or outside interests. He didn't own a pair of shorts. He played no golf. Police work sprung him out of bed every morning. There wasn't anything else.

"I'm going to plant them anyway," said Henrietta Mitchell. "Even if they don't last, what could it hurt?"

"That's the spirit,' said Vaughn.

Walking back to his car, Vaughn thought of Olga. What she was doing at that moment, where she was. Olga was probably shopping up at Wheaton Plaza, or visiting with her friends, who were Jewish gals, mostly. Sitting in one of their kitchens, smoking Silva Thins or Vantages, had the hole in the filter, drinking coffee, gossiping, or playing with those mah-jongg tiles. The Vaughns were Catholics and worshipped at St. John's near their house. Well, Olga worshipped, and Vaughn went along. As Catholic as she was, and Olga was devout, she mainly gravitated toward Jewish ladies when she wanted to socialize. Vaughn scratched his forehead. A female Jew was a Jewess, right? Olga had told him that term was old and only cavemen still used it.

Okay, Olga, whatever you say.

Picturing her lecturing him, her hand on the hip of her pedal pushers, her red, red lipstick shouting out against her pancake-white face, Vaughn smiled.

Olga was on his mind often while he worked. Much as she annoyed him when he was home, and as little romance as they had between them, she never left his head for too long. As for Linda Allen, he only thought of her when he felt a stirring in his trousers. Funny how that was.

I guess I love my wife, thought Vaughn.

Done reflecting, he got into his Dodge.

MAYBELLINE WALKER had taken Military Road off 16th and cut down Oregon Avenue. Crossing Nebraska Avenue and hanging a left on Tennyson Street, just past the Army Distaff Hall, she came to stop in front of a center-hall brick colonial in a neighborhood called Barnaby Woods.

Keeping far back, Strange pulled over to the curb near the corner of Oregon and let his Chevy idle.

Maybelline got out of her Pontiac, went to the colonial, knocked on its front door, and was soon greeted by a middle-aged white woman, who let her inside. As the door closed, Strange pulled the horseshoe shifter back into drive and drove past the house. Making note of the address, he continued on to Connecticut Avenue, where he found a pay phone on the retail strip running south of Chevy Chase Circle.

Strange phoned Lydell Blue at the Fourth District station. Lydell was pulling desk duty. It was a break for Strange.

"What's goin on, Sarge?" said Strange.

"Don't Sarge *me*."

"Got a favor to ask, blood."

"And don't blood me, either," said Blue. "Not when you looking for favors."

"Do I ask for many?"

"Matter of fact, you do. Would be nice if you called me once in a while and said, I don't know, 'Let's meet for a beer.'"

"What you want, a box of chocolates, too? You sound like a female."

"Come over here right now and this female will put a foot up your ass."

"When I do try to get you out, you say you can't."

"I got responsibilities now."

"Wasn't me who told you to get married."

"What do you know about marriage? Even if you were married, Derek, you wouldn't be."

"True." Strange wasn't proud of it. His friend Lydell knew him well. "About that favor..."

"What is it?"

Strange gave him the address he had memorized. "I need a phone number and names."

"Where can I reach you?"

"I'll hold. I *know* you got the crisscross right there."

"Gimme a minute," said Blue. Shortly thereafter, he got back on the line with the information. Strange wedged the receiver between his chin and chest as he wrote it down.

"Thanks, brother."

"That all?"

"What kind of flowers you like? I wanna send you a bouquet."

"*Fuck* you, man."

"You my boy," said Strange, and hung up the phone.

Strange had time, and he was hungry. He drove down to the Hot Shoppes on Connecticut, below Albemarle Street, sat at the counter, and ate a Teen Twist with fries and a Coke. The waitress mentioned that Mr. Isaac Hayes was across the street at the WMAL studios, doing an interview in advance of a local performance. When Strange was finished with his meal, he settled up, went outside, and stood on Connecticut Avenue. Wasn't long before Isaac Hayes came out of the building across the street and walked toward a waiting limousine. Hayes was shirtless, his big chest and shoulders draped in the multiple, thick-link gold chains he'd worn at Wattstax and on the cover of *Hot Buttered Soul*.

"Black Moses," said Strange with wonder.

He checked his watch. Reckoning that Maybelline would be in that house tutoring for another hour or so, Strange walked a half block north to the Nutty Nathan's stereo and appliance store and had a look around. A mustached salesman, pink eyed and smelling of weed, malt liquor, and breath mints, got a hold of him and promptly led him to the sound room in the back of the store, where he put an album on a BSA platter and demoed a high-amp sound system played through the much-touted Bose 901 speakers. A stinging guitar intro came forward.

Strange's eyes widened involuntarily. It was not the kind of music he normally listened to, but the sound quality of the system was outrageous and the song was blowing back his head.

"Steely Dan," said the salesman. "New group out of California."

"Nice," said Strange.

"'Your everlasting summer, you can feel it fading fast,'" said the salesman, reciting the lyrics dramatically. He hand-brushed a Hitleresque shock of black hair that had fallen across his forehead, then did some fretwork with his fingers. "They can *play*, Jim."

"The name's Derek."

"Johnny McGiness," said the salesman, extending his hand. Strange shook it. "Maybe I'll be back."

McGinnes smiled stupidly. "If I don't see you here, I'll see you ... *hear?*"

Before he left, Strange purchased a four-pack of blank Memorex tapes. A skinny young white dude, probably around sixteen, his white-boy Afro touching his shoulders, in Levi 501s rolled up cigarette-style and a Nutty Nathan's T-shirt, stood by the register counter, eyeing Strange. Had to be a stock boy, 'cause he held a dustrag in his hand. Looked like an Italian or a Greek, what with the large Mediterranean nose that dominated his face. He, too, had stoned eyes.

A female clerk with dilated pupils handed Strange the bagged-up tapes, the package no bigger than a sandwich.

The young man said, "Would you like me to take that out to your car for you, sir?"

"I think I can handle it," said Strange.

The young man smiled. "Just doin my j-o-b."

Smartass, thought Strange. And heading out the door, he

thought: Is it just me, or is everyone in this motherfucker high?

VAUGHN HAD a brief conversation with Dewight Mitchell, a D.C. Transit bus mechanic who troubleshot at the depot up by 14th and Decatur. Mitchell was about Vaughn's age, solidly built, with short gray hair and veins thick as worms on the backs of his workingman hands. Once Mitchell had shown him his Electra, a convertible, Vaughn knew for certain he was speaking to the wrong man. He had known, in fact, since he'd met Henrietta, Mitchell's wife.

They talked cars, mainly. Vaughn said he was a Mopar man but felt that Dodge had erred with the design change they'd made after the golden years of '66 and '67. Mitchell liked GMs for their elegant lines but conceded their mechanical inferiority. Said he could break down any kind of engine, so the nuts-and-bolts shortcomings didn't bother him much, long as he was driving a nice-looking car.

They shook hands and Vaughn went on his way.

In Vaughn's mind, he was straight with black people. He got along fine with them, mostly, if they were polite and close to his age. It was some of the young ones, with their attitude, who rubbed him the wrong way. As if to underscore the point, a dark guy with a blowout crossed the road up by Colorado Avenue, taking his sweet old time as Vaughn approached in his Monaco. Vaughn had to stop and wait for the young man to pass, and got an eyefuck for his courtesy. It was that special look that said, I dare you to hit me, white man.

Maybe I should pull over and kick your ass, thought

Vaughn. But these days, at the urging of Olga, he was trying to get with the program and move to a higher spiritual place, join hands with all the people of colors and step forward into the light.

Vaughn showed the spade his choppers and drove on.

FOURTEEN

FIRST THING Clarence Bowman did after reporting for work at D.C. General early that morning was to check in on Roland "Long Nose" Williams. Looking through the open door of his room, he saw an orderly changing the sheets on Roland's empty bed. Confirming that Williams had been released, Bowman called in to the home office and said he was experiencing stomach problems that rendered him unable to work. Excused from his duties for the day, he returned to his apartment off H Street, got out of his security guard uniform, and changed into triple-pleat black slacks, a gray poly shirt, black side-weaves, and a summer-weight sport jacket, also black. Bowman phoned Coco Watkins and told her that Williams was back on the street.

"I'll make sure Red gets the message," said Coco. "You on your thing?"

"I could use some female assistance," said Bowman. "Phone call shit."

"My girls are kinda shook from a bust went down last

night. You know they be delicate sometimes." Bowman heard Coco inhale deeply on a cigarette as she thought it over. "There's an all-purpose girl, goes by Gina Marie. She should be down at the diner on U. She goes there to start her day."

"I know Gina."

"Many men do," said Coco. "That girl will do anything for a dime."

Bowman ended the call. He went to his small kitchen and dropped the door on the oven of his freestanding electric range. In its cool cavity were two guns: an S&W .38 and a Colt .22. Bowman checked the loads on both and slipped them into a small gym bag. He found the keys to his Mercury Cougar and with bag in hand left out of his crib.

COCO WATKINS looked out the big window of her office-bedroom to the wide expanse of 14th Street. Down the block, near the corner of R, she saw an unmarked stripped-down white sedan carrying a side-spot, and a hand, cigaretted and draped loosely on the lip of the open driver's-side window, belonging to the cop behind its wheel. MPD had put a plainclothes officer outside her place in the event that her man would pay her a visit. She had expected that. But she had missed another street detail.

Focusing on the unmarked, Coco did not take notice of a black Continental parked on the opposite side of 14th, or the two white men who were its occupants. Had she studied the Lincoln, she would have noted that the car was not a typical police vehicle, and that the men inside it didn't look like law.

It was not like Coco to be sloppy, but she was stressed. She had spent the night in lockup, had been forced to lie down on a hard cot, and had gotten no more sleep than a cat on coffee. Then she had returned in the morning to find her place burgled and tossed. Couple of the doors of the girls' rooms had been broke off their hinges, and the pretty ring Red had given her was gone. She didn't know how she was going to tell him. Top it off, she was worried about him. She'd already heard that he'd robbed Two-Tone Ward earlier that day, and given Ward a beatdown in the bargain. That would come back on Red for sure.

Coco dressed in tight-fitting bells, low heels, and a nice silk blouse, put on some costume jewelry, and made herself up in the light of her vanity mirror. She went out into the hall and talked to Shay and a couple of the other girls who were relaxing in their rooms. Said she'd be around and would return but didn't know when. Told Shay she'd check in with her later. Reminded them that it was a work night, and to prepare themselves to get back on the stroll.

Coco used the fire escape to go down to the alley, where a boy was watching her red-over-white Fury. She gave him a five-dollar bill and fired the Plymouth up.

STRANGE WENT to a pay phone outside the Boukas Florist, high on Connecticut, and dialed the number Lydell Blue had provided for the house on Tennyson. The lady of the house, Hallie Young, answered. Strange gave her his name but not his occupation.

"I understand you're using a Miss Maybelline Walker as a math tutor," said Strange. "She's been recommended to me for my daughter."

"Yes, we hired Maybelline to help our son."

"She gave me your name as a reference." Strange figured this untruth would get back to Maybelline, but he would deal with that conflict when it arose.

"We're pleased with her, so far. She's only just made her second visit today."

"How did you come to know of her services, originally? If you don't mind my asking."

"She was referred to us by a couple we know from the neighborhood. The Rosens. Seth and Dayna live over on Thirty-First Place. Dayna used her longer than we have."

"Would you happen to have their phone number?"

"Hold on, Mr. Strange."

Strange held, and got what he was after. He hung up the phone, lifted the receiver back out of its cradle, and made his next call.

THE SECOND name on Vaughn's list took him to the neighborhood of Brightwood, off Georgia Avenue. He was looking for a Costas Lambros, who was the registered owner of a '68 gold Electra.

Lambros lived on Tuckerman Street in a small neat house of brick and shingle. A large healthy fig tree was set against the south wall of the colonial. From his years on patrol, Vaughn knew that one could identify the past and present Greek-owned homes in any community by the fig trees growing in their yards.

Vaughn inspected the Buick that was parked out front. It was a base-model Electra, stripped down and stock from the factory, with a white roof. It was a nice vehicle, but it was not a deuce.

An old man came out of the house, his pants cinched sloppily above his waist with a mangled leather belt. His wife, her gray hair tied up in a bun, wearing a housedress, orthopedic shoes, and calf-length stockings, followed. Both of them walked with difficulty. As he approached, the old man's lips were moving, but there were no sounds emanating from his mouth.

Costas and Voula Lambros wanted to know why Vaughn was standing by their car. They had to be mindful of strangers. The neighborhood had changed for the worse, what with "the *mavri*" moving in. Costas had owned a fruit-and-vegetable stand in the Eastern Market for many years, and his wife, Voula, had worked beside him. Their kids had families of their own and were living in the suburbs. Nixon had to do something soon about the welfare and all the crime.

Vaughn thanked them and apologized for taking their time. Driving away he thought, Please don't let that happen to me.

CLARENCE BOWMAN parked his Cougar on 11th, walked around the corner, and entered the diner that remained one of the few spots of thriving commerce and life on U Street since the riots.

Bowman saw Gina Marie at the counter, seated on one of its red-cushioned stools. To the left of her was another streetwalker who went by Martina. Martina was picking at a basket of fries drowning in ketchup. All the counter seats were taken, as were most of the two- and four-tops spread about the front of the house. The diner's storied jukebox was playing "Talking Loud and Saying Nothing," James

Brown's new one, Parts I and II, and hard-at-work employees and patrons alike were moving their heads to its surging, infectious groove. Bowman stood over the shoulder of a man who was sitting to the right of Gina Marie and waited. The man felt Bowman's presence, turned his head and gave him a look, then a double look, and got up off his stool, basket of lunch in hand. Bowman had a seat.

"Girl," said Bowman.

"Clarence."

From the baggage underneath her eyes, it looked like Gina Marie had just got up out of bed. She was a hard-faced woman to begin with, half used up at twenty-five. She wore a curly brown wig and false eyelashes, and a short red dress that showed off her heavily muscled legs. Reminded Bowman of that running back, Don Nottingham, played for Baltimore, the low-to-the-ground man they called "the Human Bowling Ball." Gina Marie was built like him, with a triangle. Some men liked that body type, but Bowman went for tall. Gina Marie was drinking a large sweet tea from a paper cup and smoking the life out of a cigarette.

Bowman lit one of his own. "What's goin on?"

"Guess you heard about Red."

"He dead?"

Gina Marie shook her head. "It's all over the telegraph. Him and Fonzo Jefferson robbed Sylvester Ward earlier today. They gave him an ass-whippin, too." Gina Marie dragged on her smoke and French-inhaled. "You know Two-Tone got police and politicians in his pocket. This ain't gonna be good for Red. Your boy must be losing his got-damn mind."

Bowman studied the burning menthol between his fingers.

"That homicide detective," said Gina Marie, "the one they call Hound Dog? He been askin around, too."

"You mean Vaughn."

Gina Marie made a head motion to her left. "He talked to Martina. Don't worry, Martina ain't give nothin up."

Bowman glared at Martina Lewis, a punchboard dressed and made up as a woman. Martina held Bowman's gaze for a moment, then looked away.

"Martina's cool," said Gina Marie, not liking Bowman's cold stare.

"There's somethin you can do for me," said Bowman.

"Say it."

Bowman reached into his shirt pocket, produced a slip of paper, and handed it to Gina Marie. On it was the phone number and address of assistant prosecutor Richard Cochnar. Bowman had copied it straight out of the book. The prosecutor had not even been on the job long enough, or made enough enemies, to realize that his contact information should be unlisted. He was that green.

"Cock-nar," said Gina Marie, struggling as she tried to read off the paper.

"It's *Cotch*-ner," said Bowman. "Ain't no *k* in that name."

"What you want me to do?"

"Go to that pay phone over there and call his place. Make your voice like a salesgirl or somethin. Ask to speak to the man of the house. I already know he won't be there."

"So why am I calling, then?"

"Listen to me. Whoever you talkin to gonna tell you that Cochnar's at work. So *you* ask what time he gonna be in."

Bowman dropped a dime and a nickel onto the counter. The dime spun and then rolled down flat. "Can you do that?"

Gina Marie picked up the change. She jumped down off the stool and strutted, quick and cocky, to the phone. Even in her heels, she wasn't more than five-foot-nothing.

While she made the call, Bowman looked at Martina Lewis. "Hey," he said, and chuckled low.

Gina Marie returned, smiling proudly, and hopped back up to her seat. "He gonna be home around seven."

Martina Lewis got up abruptly, walked by them, and headed out the door.

"Martina a man," said Gina Marie, apropos of nothing.

"Clarence Carter can see that shit," said Bowman, and he, too, rose up off his stool. He crushed out his cigarette, removed a ten from his wallet, and slid it in front of Gina Marie.

"Thanks, sugar," she said.

Bowman, not one to waste words, was already gone.

DAYNA ROSEN had declined to give Strange any information over the phone. He told her that he happened to be in the neighborhood and politely asked if he could stop by her place and speak with her face-to-face. After a short silence on her end of the line, she agreed. But when she got a look at him, a strong young black man walking up her sidewalk, she took him around the side of her house, one of the many center-hall brick colonials of Barnaby Woods, and had him sit on its screened back porch. She was being cautious because of his color, something she'd never admit to him or herself. But he knew.

Dayna Rosen was a dark-haired, brown-eyed woman in

her late twenties, wearing bell-bottom jeans, a leather vest, rope sandals, and a Hanoi Jane shag straight out of *Klute*. She and Strange sat on the back porch in comfortable chairs, part of an outdoor furniture set that looked like it had cost good money. She had served him iced tea. African masks hung on the porch's posts, and a Coltrane poster had been framed and mounted on the paneled outside wall. The Rosens were making a statement, and Strange took it in.

Dayna gave him a shorthand summation of their lives. Her husband, Seth, was an attorney for a labor union and he was at work. Their son, Zach, was in first grade at Lafayette Elementary. He was having a little trouble keeping up in math. They thought they'd "nip it in the bud" early and get him a tutor. Dayna had seen a flyer posted on the bulletin board at the Chevy Chase Library and she'd called the number given for Maybelline Walker, who was offering her expertise and services.

"How'd that work out?" said Strange.

"Fine," said Dayna. "What she did was helpful."

"First grade is kinda young to have a tutor isn't it?"

"Zach needed assistance." She looked him over. "How old is your daughter?"

"She's ten," said Strange recklessly. He hadn't thought the age thing through.

Dayna's eyes flickered. She glanced at his hands, which carried no wedding ring. "You and your wife must have had her at a very early age."

"I plucked my bride straight out the cradle," said Strange with a clumsy smile. "So, Maybelline Walker. You used her for how long?"

"A month, I guess. Maybe four sessions."

"Only a month?"

"Something…" She stopped, moved her eyes away from his, and finished her thought. "Something happened."

"Was there some kind of problem with her work?"

Distracted and out of sorts, Dayna got up out of her chair and used her palms to smooth out the wrinkles in her jeans. She picked up her glass, which she had barely drunk from, and said, too hurriedly, "I'm going to get some more tea. Would you like a refill?"

"I'm good," said Strange.

She was gone for a while. When she returned, she stood by the table and made no move to sit. Her jawline had hardened and there was steel in her voice. "You should go. I called the police."

"Why would you do that?"

"I don't believe you have a daughter, for one, or that you're married. You're not telling me the truth."

Strange nodded. "Sometimes, in my line of work, it's just easier to lie."

"Who are you?"

"I'm doing a background check on Maybelline Walker for a client," said Strange, telling another lie. "I'm an investigator on the private side."

"Let me see some identification."

Strange pulled his ticket from his wallet and handed it to her. "You didn't call the police, did you?"

"No, but I should have." She dropped the license in front of him on the glass table. "Please go."

"Want me to use the servants' exit?"

"What's that supposed to mean?"

"I'm sayin, Maybelline did better than I did. Least she got through the front door."

Strange pictured Dayna on some college campus, not too long ago, an enthusiastic participant in the revolution. And now, living this good life in Chevy Chase, D.C., seeing that this capitalism thing was not all that bad, but still trying to hold on to her ideals. That white guilt thing had to be heavy on her shoulders.

Strange's implied accusation cut but didn't soften Dayna. Color came to her face.

"Bullshit," she said. "Don't lay that crap on me."

"I apologize for coming here on false pretenses," said Strange.

Dayna, exasperated, sat back down in her chair. "What do you want, really? What's this *about?*"

Strange leaned forward. "You said something happened."

FIFTEEN

VAUGHN DROVE over the Anacostia River, went north on Minnesota Avenue, and turned right on one of the single-syllable streets running alphabetically across the grid of central Northeast. The block ended in a circle, with a stand of thin woods split by a ribbon of creek. Boxy brick apartment buildings, housing residents on government assistance, were visible on the other side of the woods.

Vaughn parked his Monaco in front of one of several wood-framed, dilapidated single-family homes, took his hat off the seat beside him, and placed it on his head. He walked up a buckled, weeded sidewalk to the house whose address he had written in his notebook. A woman was on the porch in a folding chair, a sweated can of Schlitz in her hand. He could see, even in her seated position, that she was tall and long of leg. Her hair hung straight. She wore a shift with open buttons up top, and her bust was full and sat high and natural. Her feet were bare. A country girl gone hard in the city.

Vaughn stopped just shy of the porch steps. "Ma'am. I'm looking for a Monique Lattimer."

Her eyes went from his head to his feet, slowly. "What kind of police are you?"

"Homicide. The name's Frank Vaughn."

"I ain't see no badge."

Vaughn showed her his shield and slipped the case back into his jacket. He could tell from her manner that courtesy would be a waste of time. Like the lawyers said, he'd have to just go ahead and treat her as hostile.

"Are you Monique?"

"Monique is me," she said, and took a swig of beer. "You got a cigarette?"

Vaughn produced his deck, shook two out of it, and made a chin motion to her porch. "I can't light you from down here."

"Come on up, then."

He took the steps to her porch. Used his lighter to fire up her cigarette, then his own, and snapped the Zippo shut. He carefully leaned his weight against a wood post that seemed to be rotting at its base.

Monique took a drag off the L&M and as she exhaled looked at the cigarette with distaste. Making it obvious that it wasn't her brand.

"According to the DMV," said Vaughn, "you're the registered owner of a sixty-eight Buick Electra."

"Yeah, it's mine."

"Gold deuce-and-a-quarter. Drop-top, right?"

"Hard."

"I don't see it."

"That's 'cause it's not here."

"Where is it, Miss Lattimer?"

She stared at the cigarette burning between her long fingers. "My brother took it this morning for a brake job."

"Took it where? A garage, something?"

"I wouldn't know. Said he had a friend was gonna work on it."

"What's your brother's name?"

"Orlando."

"Lattimer?"

"Roosevelt. Like the high school."

"Where can I find him?"

"Huh?"

"Does your brother have an address?"

"He stays with a girl over in Seat Pleasant, but I don't know where she live at, exactly."

"He got a phone number?"

"I expect he does."

"Okay," said Vaughn, taking a deep breath. "Where's your place of employment?"

"I'm between jobs at the present."

"How long you been out of work?"

"Two years, somethin like that."

"High-end Electra will run you, what, five, six thousand?"

"I bought it secondhand."

"Four grand, then. Where'd you get the bread for that much car if you're not working?"

Monique shrugged and smiled a little, as if he had said something stupid. "I got a good deal on it."

"Where?"

"Used-car lot."

"Where?"

"Shit, I don't know. Marlow Heights?"

"The dealership name would be on the title."

"Damn if I know where I put that piece of paper. It's in the house somewhere."

"Maybe I could come in and help you find it."

"If you had a warrant, you could."

"I can get one."

"Then get one."

Vaughn dragged on his cigarette and blew smoke toward Monique. It shattered when it reached her, and she did not blink.

"You know an Alfonzo Jefferson?" said Vaughn.

"Can't say I do."

"How 'bout Robert Lee Jones? Tall, light-skinned fella, goes by Red."

"Sorry."

"Aren't you going to ask me what this is about?"

"I would if I gave a fuck."

Vaughn grinned, took a last hit off his cigarette, and flicked it out onto her yard. "See you around, Monique."

"Any time."

Vaughn, energized, went back to his car and got in the driver's seat. He had a look around the street, the woods, a makeshift playground with rusted equipment, the apartment buildings on the other side of the creek. Wouldn't be hard to set up a stakeout here, but the watcher would have to be a black officer in plainclothes to blend in. Man or woman, didn't matter, but it could be done.

Vaughn smiled at Monique as he drove away, and damn if she didn't smile back. God, did he love his job.

STRANGE WENT over to Park View, drove his Monte Carlo down an alley, and parked behind the kitchen entrance to Cobb's, the fish place on Georgia. Cobb, in his bloodstained apron, was sitting on an overturned milk crate, smoking a cigarette. Strange walked through the long shadows of late afternoon, noting with satisfaction that he had put much work in today.

He approached the aged but still hard proprietor and stood beside him.

"Mr. Cobb. My name's Derek Strange. You remember me?"

Cobb squinted against the low sun. "Refresh my memory."

Strange said that he was the detective who had recently visited Cobb and asked about his former dishwasher, Bobby Odum, now deceased. Strange was wondering if Odum had ever been visited on his job site by a young woman. When Strange described her, Cobb's eyes came alive.

"Yeah, that young lady came by a couple a times."

"When I stopped by before, you said you didn't recall any of his relatives or friends."

"You ain't mention her, though," said Cobb, flicking his hot ash toward a feral cat that was crossing in front of him in the alley. The cat, keeping low to the ground, darted away. "Girl like that's hard to forget."

"What do you remember about her?"

"Her bumps. The way she walked. How her big ass jumped around in her dress." Cobb chuckled at Strange's amused expression. "That's right, young man. I might have some years on me, but that right there was choice."

"What else?"

"I saw Odum kissin on her one day, right here, outside the back door. She was lettin him, but you know, any fool could see that she wasn't into it. What I was thinking was, how'd a little man like Bobby get so much woman? 'Cause a girl like that has needs. You know what I'm talking about?"

"I do indeed," said Strange. Something rustled inside him, like a snake in dry leaves.

He, too, had needs.

VAUGHN ENTERED the offices of the Third District headquarters and went to his desk. He found a memo slip taped to his phone. Martina Lewis had called and asked that he get back to him.

Vaughn visited with Detective Charles Davis, who was on the bubble, waiting to catch his next case. Davis was a young, stylish guy, one of the few blacks in this house who had been promoted to Homicide. Vaughn felt he was friendly enough with him to ask for a favor. Davis agreed to stake out Monique Lattimer's house in exchange for something in return.

"I got you, Hound Dog," said Davis. "But I'm gonna bank this one."

"Count on it," said Vaughn.

Their supervisor, Lieutenant David Harp, tall, white, whippet thin, middle-aged, and blue-eyed, with black slicked-back hair, came into the room and told Vaughn he wanted to see him in private.

"Right now," said Harp.

Vaughn wiggled his eyebrows at Davis before following Harp back to his office. The white shirts rarely bothered him, and when they did he didn't let it get under his skin. He wasn't bucking for promotion. He already had the job he wanted. The only way they could hurt him was to fire him, and they'd never do that. Vaughn's closure rate was top-shelf.

Harp was already behind his desk when Vaughn walked into the office. Vaughn took the hot seat, a hard chair set in front of Harp's desk. He removed his hat, held it in his lap, and waited.

"Where you been, Detective?"

"Working my case. The Odum homicide."

"The suspect is Robert Lee Jones, correct?"

Vaughn nodded. "Street name Red. We just need to put the bracelets on him. Charles Davis is gonna stake out a woman who'll lead us to Alfonzo Jefferson, Jones's partner. We're close."

"I've been tryin to get hold of you. You take your personal car today?"

"I'm more comfortable in my own vehicle, sir."

"It has a two-way in it, doesn't it?"

"Yes, sir," said Vaughn. "But sometimes I forget and leave it off." Truth was, he didn't like to be bothered with the constant crackle of the radio while he was doing his job. The talk over the police frequency almost never had a thing to do with him.

Harp drew a pencil from a leather cup and tapped it on his desk. "Your boy Red and his partner robbed Sylvester Ward in his own house. Happened this morning. Y'know that?"

"First I heard of it," said Vaughn. He was intrigued, but he tried not to let his emotions play out on his face.

"Know who Ward is?"

"That would be Two-Tone Ward. The numbers man."

"Correct. He reported the crime soon as it happened. But Ward didn't call the MPD. He called his city councilman. And the mayor, for all I know. And then *I* got calls. More than one. Matter of fact, these politicians have been up my ass all day. They want to know when we're gonna get this joker off the street."

"I'm sorry about the trouble it caused you, sir. If you want me to explain the progress of my case to any of those gentlemen—"

"*Fuck* them."

"Yes, sir." Vaughn smoothed out the brim of his hat. "It's unusual for a guy like Ward to call the authorities, even after he's been victimized. I mean, there's a code."

"They broke it. Red and his partner beat Ward like an animal before they left his house. From what I hear, Ward wasn't even resisting."

"Sounds like my man."

"What's this guy's problem?"

"Red Jones isn't looking forward to retirement or old age, Lieutenant. He's living for this summer. Today. People all over the city are talking about him. The notoriety pours gasoline on his fire. That's what he wants."

Harp slipped the pencil back into its cup. He relaxed his shoulders and sat back in his chair. "Bring the mother-fucker in."

"Bet it," said Vaughn.

"And keep your radio on, Detective."

Walking out of the offices, Vaughn put his hand in his pocket and touched a slip of paper. It was the message from Martina Lewis.

SIXTEEN

STRANGE STOOD on a landing in an apartment building on 15th Street, located across the road from Malcolm X Park. He made a fist and prepared to knock on the door before him. He hesitated, knowing he could still go back down the stairs. Knowing he was wrong. There were many ways a young man could ruin things with a good woman, and this was the most thoughtless. But he was here, right now, and he had come here deliberately and with determination. Later, if confronted, he would make excuses, but there weren't any valid ones, none for real. He wanted what he wanted. He had been thinking on it since the woman had walked into his office, swinging her hips.

Strange recalled the day he had sat at the Three-Star Diner when his father, Darius, was still alive and working the grill. Seeing a moment pass between his father and the Three-Star's longtime waitress, Ella. Recognizing the familiar look between them that suggested intimacy and maybe even love. He had always thought that his mother and father had shared an unbreakable, sacred bond. To realize, at that moment, that his father had cheated, and had done so, perhaps, for many years, had dropped Strange's heart. But it hadn't ruined Darius in Strange's eyes.

Much as he loved his mother, Strange couldn't bring himself to righteous anger or to hate his father for his transgression. Yes, he was disappointed. Also, he understood. His father, like all mortals, was a sinner, fallible. In matters of the flesh he was downright weak.

I am my father, thought Strange, as he knocked on Maybelline Walker's door. No better than any other man. Just a man.

VAUGHN BOUGHT a ticket at the Lincoln box office and went through the lobby to the auditorium. The 5:30 show was about to begin. *Buck and the Preacher* had been held over, but first the projectionist was running a reel of trailers for the current features playing at other District Theaters, a chain whose bookers programmed films for black audiences in black neighborhoods. Vaughn let his eyes adjust and watched the promo for *The Legend of Nigger Charley*, currently running down at the Booker T. *How the West Was Rewritten*, thought Vaughn, as he spotted Martina in one of the middle rows and made his way to a seat beside him.

"Just got your message, baby," said Vaughn, leaning close to Martina so he could keep his voice low and still be heard.

"You weren't followed or nothin, were you?" Martina was wearing a dress, heels, and red lipstick.

"No. This about Red Jones? 'Cause I already know about the Sylvester Ward robbery."

"That's not why I called you."

"I gotta find Red. Get me his location and I'll make it worth your while."

"Money," said Martina huskily, with a dismissive wave of his hand. "Cash ain't gonna do nothing for me unless you got a lot *of* it."

"Tell me what's going on."

In the light coming from the screen, Martina's features were angular, masculine, and troubled.

"Tell me," said Vaughn.

"Hitter name of Clarence Bowman came into the diner earlier today. Was talkin to Gina Marie."

"I know Gina."

"Many do. Bowman had Gina Marie call some woman up on the phone and ask her when her man was gonna be home tonight. I had the impression that Bowman was about to put work in."

"*What* man?"

"A prosecutor. Cotch-somethin."

"Cochnar?"

"That's what it was."

Vaughn wrapped a hand around Martina's forearm, hard as wood. "What's Bowman look like?"

"Tall, dark, and cut. Like that actor, used to be an athlete."

Vaughn looked at the screen, saw Fred Williamson, and said, "Him?"

"Nah, one of them Olympic dudes."

"I gotta get out of here."

"Wait a minute, Frank."

"We'll settle up later."

"It's not about that," said Martina, looking at him straight on. "I'm scared."

"Keep it together," said Vaughn. "I'll work it out. You'll be fine."

Vaughn rose abruptly and rushed up the auditorium aisle. Martina's head jerked birdlike around the house. He was trying to see if anyone had been watching or listening to their conversation. Half-believing that they had not been observed, Martina slouched in his seat and got low.

DEREK STRANGE sat in a big cushiony armchair in the living room of Maybelline Walker's apartment, the last of the day's sun coming in through her west-wall windows. Maybelline sat on a matching sofa, so close to him that her bare knee almost touched his. She was in her strapless dress and she had removed her shoes. Her big natural was lifted by the wind of a floor fan set near the furniture. It was warm running to hot in her pad. Both of them were drinking Miller High Lifes out of bottles. Beads of sweat had formed on Maybelline's forehead and across her chest, where the tops of her breasts were exposed. Strange could smell her perspiration and that sweet strawberry scent he remembered from the time she had visited his office.

Maybelline had put the Staple Singers' *Be Altitude: Respect Yourself,* their new one on the Stax label, on her compact system, and Mavis was belting out "This Old Town (People in This Town)," the last track on side one.

Strange and Maybelline were deep into their conversation. It had become a confession for her. She claimed it felt good to get it out. Now that the horse had been let out the barn, Maybelline had begun to drop her finishing-school manner of speech, and her *G*'s.

"Hallie Young phoned me just after you gave her a call," said Maybelline, giving Strange a wicked eye, "askin for references."

"That *was* kind of lame of me," said Strange. "And then I really messed up when I met that Rosen gal. Told her I was looking for a tutor for my ten-year-old daughter."

"Your look doesn't say 'devoted father.' Or husband."

"I'm too young," said Strange. "Ain't nobody gonna tie me down to a marriage. Not yet."

They both sipped at their beers.

"How'd you find the ring?" said Strange.

Maybelline wiped a bit of foam from her full mouth. "Dayna Rosen used to leave me with her son alone in that house for, like, two hours at a time."

"She barely knew you."

"Derek, she didn't know me at *all*. But white folks like her, they just overdo that 'I feel for your people' thing. Tryin so hard to be right. Like, Look at me, I got an actual black person in my home, and I'm gonna trust her enough to leave her there *with my child* while I run errands around town. If I had a kid, I wouldn't leave it with a stranger, would you?"

"We already established I don't have one, so I can't answer that."

"Dayna used to call me *girl*, *sister*, all that jive. Shoot, she was no kin to me."

Strange, trying to redirect her, said, "Back to the ring."

"Dayna had showed it to me, and then I saw it again in a jewelry box in their master bedroom one day while she had gone out and Zachary had disappeared. I was always having to go and look for him. Boy couldn't sit still and work on math to save his life."

"Six years old, he's not supposed to sit still."

"I didn't steal that ring," said Maybelline.

"I know," said Strange. "Bobby Odum did."

Maybelline's eyes went to the beer bottle in her hand. "I had got to know Bobby. Used to go into Cobb's for my fish sandwich, and he'd come out from the kitchen every time he saw me walk through the door. We went out for a drink, and he mentioned his history…"

"Odum was a second-story man, among other things. You put him up to the burglary, right?"

"Yes," she said, turning her face away suddenly, like an actress in a silent film. "He volunteered to steal it, once I told him about the ring."

"Why would he do that?"

"I didn't have to get with him, if that's what you mean."

"Cobb said he saw you two lockin lips out back his shop."

"Kissin ain't fuckin."

"It can have the same effect."

"I'm not above letting a man give me a kiss to get where I need to be."

"So you didn't sleep with him."

"Please," said Maybelline. "Do I look like the kind of woman that Bobby Odum could satisfy?"

"I don't blame him for trying. After all, he was a man."

"He wasn't much of one."

Strange studied her. "The Rosens did you a solid by hiring you. Didn't you feel any, you know, remorse?"

"Not really. Dayna didn't pay a dime for that ring. That day when she had it on her hand, she said herself that it came down from her grandmother, like an inheritance."

"When Dayna and her husband realized it had been stolen, they did what?"

"They called the police," said Maybelline with a shrug. "The night Bobby stole it, the Rosens were all out to dinner somewhere, and the house was locked up. If they suspected me as an accomplice, they kept it to themselves. I guess they didn't want to jam up another young black woman with the law. I swear, sometimes I felt like I could have slapped that woman in the face and she would have apologized to *me*."

Strange recalled his conversation with Dayna Rosen. She'd said that she had told Maybelline they would no longer require her services, using the excuse that progress had been made with Zach and the job was complete. She had never accused Maybelline of anything and had even defended her, in a way, to Strange. Strange felt that the Rosens were decent people, if hugely naive. Maybelline saw their kindness as stupidity.

"What about the police?" said Strange.

"Police never even questioned me. You know the MPD don't do shit for follow-up on those burglaries."

The music had come to an end. Maybelline put her bottle down on a glass coffee table and went to her stereo. She took the album off the platter, replaced it in its sleeve, found a 45, and fitted a plastic adaptor into its center space. She dropped the record onto the spindle of the turntable and flipped the play lever located on the side of the platter. Luther Ingram's new smash, "(If Loving You Is Wrong) I Don't Want to Be

Right," came forward. Ordinarily, Strange would have thought, Koko 2111. He would have if he had not been studying Maybelline's lush figure filling out every inch of her dress.

"You still buying singles?" said Strange.

"That's all they had at the record store," said Maybelline, and she went back to the sofa and sat on one end of it. She patted the empty portion of the cushion. "Why you sittin so far away?"

"Am I?"

"You could have phoned me," she said. "I know you didn't come over here to give me a personal update."

"How you know why I came over? You got ESP?"

"Derek, I believe you're scared."

Fightin words, thought Strange. And: Figures that a mathematics teacher would have it all worked out. Everything this woman does is calculation.

He didn't even like Maybelline Walker. But he moved to the sofa and sat beside her.

"That's better," she said.

She reached across him and held his hand.

"You still gonna find that ring for me?"

"I take a job," said Strange, "I see it through."

She moved his hand and placed it on her chest. Strange slipped his fingers inside the fabric of her dress and cupped her left tit. He brushed her nipple, pinched it, and felt it swell. She shifted her body into his and they kissed. Her flesh was warm beneath his touch and their tongues danced and he grew hard. Her legs parted and his hand went between them and she was naked there. She moaned as he found her spot and stroked her slick divide.

"God*damn*," she said.

"What?"

"Come *on*."

As quickly as he had been sprung, Strange lost his desire. He sat back on the couch. The image of Carmen had flashed in his mind, but it wasn't just his conscience that had thrown cold water on his intent. After all, he'd been unfaithful to Carmen before; because of his nature, he would probably cheat again. But not today.

Strange slowly got to his feet. He straightened out his shirt and adjusted himself inside the crotch of his bells.

"What the fuck is wrong with you?" said Maybelline.

"You talk too much," said Strange.

COCO WATKINS, Red Jones, and Alfonzo Jefferson sat on comfortable furniture around a cable spool table set up in the living room of Jefferson's bungalow in Burrville. They were drinking beer from clear longnecked bottles and passing around a fat joint of herb. Jefferson had copped an OZ of premium Lumbo with his cut of the money they'd taken off Sylvester Ward. "Walk from Regio's," an instrumental from the *Shaft* soundtrack, was coming from the stereo, and Jefferson was moving his head to its bass, key, and woodwind vamp.

"This is bad right here," said Jefferson, his woven hat cocked on his head, his eyes close to bleeding. "You *know* Isaac's in town tonight."

"We got plans," said Coco, eyeing Jefferson with annoyance.

"I know," said Jefferson, and he smiled with sympathy at

Jones. "Donny and Roberta. Sounds like a real house party. You can't dance to that shit, though. It's got no backbeat."

Jones hit the joint, hit it again, and handed it to Jefferson. When Jones spoke, smoke came with his words. "What'd your woman say, exactly?"

"Monique? Said Vaughn came by, lookin for my Buick. Registration and title's got her name on it."

"Ward snitched us out to the law. I can't believe it."

"Ain't no honor out here anymore." Jefferson inspected the burning herb, wrapped loosely in Top papers, and drew on it deep.

"Where your deuce at now?" said Jones.

"Parked in my yard, out back. Can't nobody see it from the street."

"If they walked into the alley they could."

Jefferson put his hand on the worn .38 that lay on the cable spool table. "Official Police" was stamped on its barrel, and he liked that. He touched its grip, wrapped in black electrical tape. "If someone walks into that alley and they look at my shit? It's on. At that point, don't nothin matter, anyway."

"How close you think Hound Dog is?"

Jefferson shrugged. "Man said our names to Monique."

"Dude stays on it," said Jones with admiration. He was not concerned. In fact, his blood ticked pleasantly. "I wouldn't go out, I was you."

"*You* about to go out."

"I gotta take care of Long Nose."

"*And* we got a date," said Coco.

"You know where Roland at?" said Jefferson.

"Soul House," said Jones. "According to you."

"If he's out the hospital, that's where he'll be."

"So you gonna stay in," said Jones pointedly. "Right?"

"Monique comin over here," said Jefferson with an idiotic grin. "Conjugal visit."

"What if she gets followed?"

"I ain't stupid," said Jefferson, smiling stupidly, his eyes gone. "Neither is Nique. She's not goin *any* goddamn where unless it's clear."

They smoked the joint down to a roach and finished their beers. Jones got up quickly from his chair. His new Rolex had slid up his forearm, and he shook it to rest on his wrist.

"Let's go, girl," he said, standing tall. He was dressed for the night in rust-colored bells, three-inch stacks, and a print rayon shirt opened to show the top of his laddered stomach. Coco, similarly fly and regal, came and stood beside him.

"You gonna take my short?" said Jefferson.

"That Buick's on fire," said Jones. "We'll be good in Coco's ride."

Jefferson liked that jam "No Name Bar," the one with all the horns, on another side of Isaac's double-record set. As Jones and Coco left the house, he found the slab of wax he was looking for and put it on.

SEVENTEEN

ROLAND WILLIAMS sat on a stool at the stainless steel bar of Soul House, his regular place on 14th. There were few patrons here, but this was not unusual. It was a dark, bare-wall space that served more men than woman, and hardly ever did so in great numbers. It was not frequented by the hip crowd, but rather by city dwellers who liked their alcohol and conversation drama free. The jukebox played cuts by the likes of Big Maybelle, Carl "Soul Dog" Marshall, Johnny Adams, and other artists whose sound had that below-the-Mason-Dixon-line vibe.

Soul House was not to be confused with the House of Soul carryout on the 2500 block of the same street, but often it was, so many simply called this spot the House. Williams thought of it as his night residence. Right now, a beautiful, bitter Ollie and the Nightingales song, "Just a Little Over-come," was playing, and Tommy Tate's vocals were powering through the room.

Williams was drinking Johnnie Walker Red, rocks. At the moment he was alone.

He was feeling poorly, but he was not low. In the hospital he had been given methadone, and he left with a prescription, but methadone was not heroin or even morphine, which is to say that it did not give him the same kind of rush. It would have to do until he could put some coin together and cop, go back to his life as he had known it, and his habit. Course, he didn't think of his drug use as an addiction, as he had always had it under control. Far as his vocation went, he had lied to the detective about putting his old self behind him, but that's what you did when you talked to the police, you lied and denied. He had a good business going; he wasn't going to drop it and move on. Move on to what?

What he wanted behind him was the violence and the hurt. He shouldn't have lipped off to Red Jones. He knew that mistake was on him, and the bullet that had passed through him was a hot warning that could have been fatal, a lesson he'd needed to learn. Wasn't his fault that the white man from up north had put the hurting on him in his hospital bed, but that awful pain was a memory now, too. The Italians would go back to New Jersey or wherever they were from, and Red, well, he would soon be in lockup or shot dead in the street, because that was how it always ended for men like him, wasn't any third choice. And he, Roland Williams, could reestablish his business and rediscover his peace.

"Another one," said Williams to the bartender, a man named Gerard who had wide shoulders and a mustache so thin it was barely holding on to his face.

"On me," said Gerard, pulling the red-labeled bottle off

the middle of the shelf and free-pouring into a fresh glass he'd filled with ice.

Williams was now known as the man who'd been shot by Jones and lived to walk back into the spot. "Long Nose caught some lead from Red Fury," he'd heard one dude say with admiration, and for once Williams didn't mind the sound of his nickname. That kind of notoriety was worth a drink on the house. He sure wasn't going to turn it down.

Gerard served it and took the empty off the bar. A woman named Othella walked behind Williams and brushed his back with her hand as she passed. She wore tight slacks the color of vanilla ice cream and an electric-blue blouse.

"Hey, Roland," she said in a singsong way.

"Where you off to, girl?"

Othella stopped and pointed a red-nailed finger at the heavy man seated on a stool by the front door. "Gotta tell Antoine somethin."

"Is Antoine your George?"

"No!"

"Then come on back and sit when you're done."

"In a minute," she said.

Roland Williams, relaxed in his surroundings and happy to be home, had a taste of scotch. He closed his eyes and let the liquor make love to his head.

CLARENCE BOWMAN parked his Cougar on 13th and Otis Street, Northeast, near Fort Bunker Hill Park. Gathering his guns, he slipped the .38 into the side pocket of his black sport jacket and wedged the .22 under the rear waistband of his slacks. He then walked south, toward Newton.

The neighborhood of Brookland held a mixture of blacks and whites, working- and middle-class, employed at the nearby Catholic University, at the post office, in the service industry, or in civil service positions downtown. Bowman, a black man in clean, understated clothing, did not stand out.

On Newton he approached the Cochnar residence, a Dutch Colonial with wood siding set on a rise. Rick Cochnar's green Maverick was parked out front. The young prosecutor was home.

Bowman looked around. Dusk had come and gone, and night had fallen on the street.

It would have been better to have caught Cochnar arriving. Bowman could have walked right up to the Ford and ended the man before he got out the driver's seat. But coming up on him like that was a hard thing to time, and it wasn't safe or smart to hang out on a residential block for too long, even if Bowman did blend in.

He'd have to do it a different way. Go up to the house, get in, and get it done quick. Better yet, coax the man outside. Most likely, Cochnar's wife was in that house, too. That was a problem for Bowman. He wasn't one of those robot killers, what they called ice men. He took out the target, not the loved ones. He'd never finished a woman or a kid. He went to church on Sundays, sometimes. There was work he wouldn't do.

Bowman went up the concrete steps that led to the Cochnar residence. Now he was on the high ground and could see inside the house. Its well-lit interior and his location gave him a prime view. On the first floor, a blond lady with a good figure was walking around a room that had a set of furniture and shelves holding books. The window he was looking through was a sash and it was wide open; he could hear a television set playing in there, too. Bowman recognized the music, the theme from that squares' program played in repeats on Channel 5. *The Lawrence Welch Show*, something like that.

Standing there, Bowman wondered, Why would a young lady like her be watching that bullshit? And if she was watching, why was the volume up so loud? Maybe the bitch was deaf. But if she was deaf, why have the sound on at all?

The tip of a gun barrel pressed behind his ear.

"Hey, shitbird," said a voice. "I'm a police officer. You do anything else besides raise your hands, I'll squeeze one off in your head. I won't even think about it. And I'll sleep good tonight."

Bowman raised his hands.

"Anne!" The man holding the gun on him shouted toward the house, and soon a bright light illuminated the porch. The woman Bowman had seen in the living room came outside, followed by a male cop in uniform. A badge was clipped to the woman's trousers, and there was a revolver in her hand. Her police sidearm was pointed at his midsection as she descended the porch steps.

"We got him," said Officer Anne Honn. She and the uniform covered Bowman with their weapons.

"Keep your hands up," said Vaughn, holstering his .38. "Don't twitch." Vaughn found Bowman's guns and inspected them in the light. "Shaved numbers. The DA's gonna like that."

"Lawyer," said Bowman.

"You're gonna need one, Hoss," said Vaughn. "Put your hands behind your back."

Bowman thought on who had set him up as he felt the bracelets lock onto his wrists. Couldn't be that punch Gina Marie, 'cause she wouldn't sign her own death certificate like that. It had to be that man-ho, called hisself Martina, who had been sitting beside Gina in the diner. Bowman needed to get a message to Red.

"Let's go," said Vaughn. With the uniformed officer beside him, Vaughn grabbed Bowman roughly by the arm and led him to a squad car that was parked around the corner in the alley. Officer Honn placed Bowman's guns in an evidence bag and went back into the house to talk to Cochnar and his wife, safely stashed in their second-story bedroom.

"You must be Vaughn," said Bowman, getting a look at the big dog-toothed white man for the first time.

"*Detective* Vaughn." He studied Bowman's face. "Damn, you do look like that actor, used to be a big-time athlete... Woody Strode, right?"

It's Rafer Johnson, thought Bowman. But he didn't bother to correct the man. He wouldn't know the difference anyhow.

COCO WATKINS pulled the Fury over to the curb in front of Soul House on 14th.

Red Jones said, "Leave it run." He pulled his guns from under the seat and chambered rounds into both of them. Pushed his hips forward as he fitted the Colts in the dip of his bells.

Coco threw the shifter into park. The 440 rumbled and sputtered through dual pipes. Coco looked to the sidewalk, where a man with a gray beard sat on a folding chair. In his hand was a bottle wrapped in a brown paper bag.

"There goes witness one," said Coco. "You 'bout to kill him, too?"

"Old-time don't bother me."

"Be better if we waited for Williams to go somewhere alone."

"Better for who?"

"You. Your future."

"I'm already wanted for murder."

"*I'm* not."

"You know how the lawyers do. They only gonna charge me for one. The one they got the best chance of taking to conviction."

"So you gonna give 'em a choice."

"What, you scared?"

"Concerned for you don't make me scared."

Jones looked over at his woman, her hair touching the headliner of the Plymouth, her red lipstick, her violet eye shadow, the nice outfit she had on. Coco always looked good when she stepped out the door. She was a stallion.

"I'm goin in there," said Jones. "You can leave me here if you want to. I'll understand. And I'll be all right."

"You think I'd leave you?" Her eyes had grown heavy. She brushed tears away with her thumbs, carefully, so as not to disturb her makeup.

Jones could see that he'd cut her. He leaned across the seats and kissed her on the mouth. "You're my bottom, girl."

Jones got out of the Plymouth and closed its passenger door behind him. He adjusted the grips of the .45s so that they pointed inward; now he could draw the way he had so many times before in the mirror. Brazenly, he tucked the tails of his rayon shirt behind the grips, so all could now see his intent.

The man sitting on the folding chair was bold behind his drink and did not take his eyes off Jones as the tall man took long strides over the sidewalk. Jones pushed on the front door of Soul House and stepped inside.

The doorman, a fat man named Antoine, took in Jones, strapped with double automatics, standing in the entrance area, surveying the space. Antoine had crossed paths with Jones once before.

"You can't bring that iron in here," said Antoine weakly, and then thought better of his tone. "Sayin, you *shouldn't*."

Jones didn't reply. Instead, he scanned the low-lit room. He focused on the back of a man seated at the bar. The man turned his head to talk to the girl beside him, revealing his fucked-up beak.

The jukebox was playing an old song, a soul thing by some blue-gum singer from out the South. Jones did not hear it. The song in his head was new, like one of those soundtrack songs they played in the movies he'd seen at the Republic, the Langston, the Senator, and the Booker T. The song in his head had one of those scratchy guitar riffs, wacka-wacka-*wacka*-wak, and a female vocal, the girl speaking, not singing, almost with a breathy kind of whisper. And now Red Jones was in the movie, crossing the barroom floor, people murmuring, moving out his way. Nearing Williams, he stopped and stood behind him. Jones could hear music and the lyrics, which went

Red Fury, he's the *man*
Try and stop him if you *can*

and Jones cross-drew his guns. He said, "Long Nose," and
as Roland Williams swiveled his barstool around, a look of
sad resignation came upon his face, and Jones fired both of
his .45s. The Colts jumped in his hands, and the girl beside
Williams screamed as gunshots thundered in the room and
the blood of Williams speckled her. Williams, leaded multiple times, toppled off his stool and fell, dead as JFK, to the
floor.

Jones's ears were ringing some. A few patrons had backed
off into the shadows and some were outright cowering, their
arms wrapped around themselves, their chins tucked into
their chests. Othella, the girl next to Williams, was frozen
where she sat, her vanilla-colored slacks darkened at the
crotch with urine. Gerard the bartender had raised his
hands without being asked to, and they were shaking. Jones,
guns still in hand, turned around and walked away. Antoine
the doorman was no longer at his post, and Gerard watched
Jones through the gun smoke as he pushed on the door and
left the bar.

Out on 14th Street, Jones got into the passenger seat of
the Fury.

"Everything all right?" said Coco.

"Straight," said Jones. His eyes were bright as he looked at
his woman. "I wrote a song about me while I was in there.
Call it my 'Ballad of Red.'"

"For *real*."

"Need to work on it some. But yeah."

Coco pulled off the curb and drove north. The juicer sitting outside Soul House watched the red Plymouth cruise away. The big-haired lady behind the wheel had left no rubber on the road. Didn't seem to him like she was in any kind of hurry at all.

That night, for days to come, and into the years, the man in the folding chair and the patrons and employees of the bar would talk about the event that had just gone down. The details would change, the roles of the witnesses would get inflated, and the story would grow to legend fueled by drama, exaggeration, and outright fabrication.

Red Jones had earned his myth.

EIGHTEEN

NEWS OF the Soul House shooting spread quickly and soon reached the Third District headquarters, where Vaughn had booked Clarence Bowman for firearms violations and secured him in a holding cell. The jail was crowded that evening, as welfare checks had recently hit the street. The sudden infusion of cash into the city initiated an increase of alcohol and drug use, which led to incidents of mayhem and domestic violence.

Bowman shared a cell with several men, some who would be arraigned shortly on serious offenses. One of the men was a doe-eyed alcoholic named Henry Arrington, in on a public drunk charge, who would be released the next morning. Bowman immediately marked Arrington as the crippled calf of the bunch. He cut Arrington from the herd, took him aside, and had a quiet but firm talk. Spoke slow, 'cause Arrington was a little off his ass on alcohol. Asked Arrington who he loved the most in this world, and Arrington said his grandmother. He then told Arrington that he would find his grandma and murder her if Arrington did not do exactly as Bowman said. Didn't matter if Bowman was going to be incarcerated for the next five, ten, or twenty years. When he got out, he would kill her dead and then he would do Arrington for fun. Bowman, of course, didn't off innocents, and it gave him no pleasure to make these threats, but he felt he had to do so in the interest of time.

"Here's the phone number," said Bowman, and had Arrington say it back to him several times.

Vaughn had been summoned to another meeting with Lieutenant David Harp back in Harp's office. This one was less cordial than the last. The brazen nature of the Soul House burn had put Harp over the edge. As the lieutenant spoke, veins stood out like hot wires on his neck. The message was clear: Red Jones was on a murderous crime spree in the city and it was Vaughn's responsibility to put it to an end. His shield depended on it. Vaughn knew the threat was bullshit, but it angered him to hear it just the same.

Vaughn returned to his desk to retrieve a fresh deck of L&Ms before heading down to the crime scene on 14th. From back in the holding cells, Vaughn could hear Clarence Bowman's agitated shouts, nonsense declarations strung together somewhat randomly: "I'm not me! I'm not myself today! My stomach hurts! I gotta make some dookie! Tellin y'all, I gotta take a *shit!*"

On the way out the door, Vaughn got up with the sergeant, Bill Herbst, who was on desk duty.

"What's Bowman's malfunction?" said Vaughn.

"He's been screaming his black ass off for the last fifteen minutes," said Herbst with a shrug.

"Sorry to leave him with you, Billy. I gotta get outta here."

"We'll deal with it, Hound Dog."

Vaughn, usually cool, now visibly shaken, lit a cigarette and tossed the match on the floor. The sergeant watched him go.

In his cell, Bowman dropped his slacks around his ankles, squatted, and shat loudly and voluminously on the concrete floor. What he did next caused alarm and activity, and sent his cell mates scattering to the farthest reaches of the iron cage. Some yelled for their jailers to get them out of there, and one hardened criminal puked up his dinner. Bowman had scooped up a handful of his bowel movement and put it into his mouth.

Bowman wasn't crazy. He was logical. It was easier to bust out of St. Elizabeth's than it was the D.C. Jail.

LOU FANELLA and Gino Gregorio had sat on Coco Watkins's house for hours. Tired and frustrated, they returned to the room of their motor lodge in Prince George's County, took naps, got up out of bed, changed into rayon print sport shirts and no-belt slacks, and found a place on Kenilworth that served Mexican.

"This joint stinks," said Fanella, shaking his head as he took the last bite of his enchilada platter. "What's the name of this shithouse again?"

"Mi Casa," said Gregorio.

"Me *Caca* is more like it."

Gregorio noted that Fanella had cleaned his plate as thoroughly as a dog would tongue-polish its bowl, but Fanella told him he was only getting his money's worth. He also told Gino to shut his mouth.

Fanella suggested they find some women. He was a man with elemental needs.

He phoned their boy, Thomas "Zoot" Mazzetti, who told him where they could buy some tail. Fanella didn't want to spend much, wasn't interested in those overpriced escort services, and anyway, those stuck-up gals weren't any fun. Zoot said the 14th and U Street corridor still had women out on the stroll.

"I don't want no monkeys," said Fanella.

"Don't worry, Lou," said Zoot. "They got white snatch down there, too."

Fanella and Gregorio got into the Lincoln and headed into the city. Reaching their general destination, they pulled over on 14th and let the Continental idle. Fanella rested his smoking-hand on the lip of the open driver's-side window as he had a look at the scene.

They were in a commercial and residential district gone to seed. There weren't a whole lot of straight citizens out, but there was life. People moving about furtively in the darkened doorways of shuttered businesses, heroin addicts, pushers, hookers, a guy dressed outrageously in a purple suit and hat, the Halloween version of a pimp. They had both noticed the unusual number of police cars cruising the area, too.

"We shouldn't stay too long, Lou," said Gregorio.

"Relax," said Fanella. "Here comes somethin now."

A black girl, low to the ground and tarted up, approached their car.

"You datin tonight, sugar?" she said, her hand on the roof of the Lincoln as she leaned in.

"We got something specific in mind."

"You police?"

"No."

"You want black girls, right?"

"White girls," said Fanella, holding up two fingers. He dragged on his cigarette and blew some smoke in her direction.

"Wait up," said the girl sourly.

A few minutes later two young white girls in their late teens walked down the sidewalk. One wore short shorts and a scoop-neck shirt with a glittery star on it stretched tight across her full chest. Her hair was on the orange side of blond. The other one was skinny, small-breasted, brunette, and wore a miniskirt and V-neck top.

"I know which one you want," said Fanella with a smile. Gino liked them slim to bony.

"So?"

"She looks like a boy."

The girls reached their car. Neither of them lived in the neighborhood of pretty, but they would do.

The one who had the woman's body looked down at Fanella. "You two datin?"

"Yeah, and we're not police. Get in the car."

"Don't you want a room?"

"I don't do whorehouses. We got a place. Let's go there and party."

"Me and my friend don't have that kind of time."

"I'll pay for your time. Get in."

The girls opened the suicides and climbed into the Lincoln. Fanella asked them their names, and the one who was doing all the talking said hers was April. The skinny trick called herself Cindy.

"I'm Lou and this is Gino."

"You got anything to drink, Lou?"

"Liquor and setups."

"I like rose-A. Cindy does, too."

"We'll get some wine, then."

"How 'bout a little blow to go with it?" said April.

"What do I look like, Rockefeller?"

"C'mon, Lou, let's have some fun."

After some negotiation, they agreed on a price. April had Fanella drive to a nearby row house on T and told him to keep the Lincoln running while she went inside. She returned a few minutes later with the eager, optimistic look of a coke addict who has just copped.

Fanella drove east as Gregorio found a radio station that April and Cindy liked. A hit song was playing, and the girls sang along to the title refrain every time it came around.

" 'Alone again'…" sang April.

"…'Naturally,'" sang Cindy and April in unison, and both of them laughed.

It was annoying, but Fanella did not tell them to knock it off. They seemed to be enjoying themselves, and that was all right with him. After all, they weren't much more than kids.

STRANGE SHOWERED, dressed in a nice slacks-and-shirt arrangement, and picked up Carmen at her apartment off Barry Place, near the playing fields across from Howard University. Carmen wore a simple, flattering minidress with hoop earrings. Her makeup was understated and just right. When she got into the passenger bucket of his Monte Carlo, they kissed. Pulling back, her eyes dimmed somewhat as she said, "You smell sweet."

"I cleaned myself up real good for you, girl," said Strange, his voice sounding unconvincing to his own ears.

He told her to find something on the radio, and she dialed it over to WOL. The station was spinning light tunes that women liked when they were alone and men and women liked to listen to when they were together. "Betcha by Golly, Wow," by the Stylistics, "Lean on Me," by Bill Withers, the 5th Dimension's "(Last Night) I Didn't Get to Sleep at All." It was like the DJ knew that they were on a date. Strange drove west, windows down, a nice pre-summer night in D.C., Carmen humming along to the music, somewhat distant maybe, but seemingly content.

Strange went to the big lot off 16th Street at Carter Barron and found a space near the amphitheater set in the woods of Rock Creek Park. He and Carmen walked with the moving crowd of stylishly dressed black Washingtonians down an asphalt path, past the box office, and through the turnstiles, where Strange presented his tickets. They found their seats in the bowl, under a clear night showcasing stars. The amphitheater had been built on a slope, designed so that the sound would reach all spaces equally, and there were few undesirable seats in the house. Strange felt that there was no better outdoor venue in the city to watch a musical performance. He reached for Carmen's hand.

Roberta Flack and Donny Hathaway had been students

together at Howard, and Flack had played piano and sang for years at the Clyde's bar, making them hometown heroes. Flack in particular received a raucous ovation as she took the stage, wearing one of several gowns she would change into during the show.

The Carter Barron engagement had been booked and sold out for several consecutive nights. The evening's program had Flack and Hathaway executing solo sets and also playing together. It was expected that they would do "Where Is the Love," their number one single on the R&B charts, and when they launched into it, a great reception was issued from the overcapacity crowd.

In truth, Strange was not much of a Roberta Flack fan. Her vibe was too soft for him, and though he would never tell Carmen, he felt it was music for females. But he found himself getting into her performance. She had an accomplished group of musicians backing her up, and her man on guitar, Eric Gale, doled out some tasty licks. Strange had seen Hathaway at the Ed Murphy's Supper Club, where he played often, and he put Donny's debut album, *Everything Is Everything*, in the category of classic. When Hathaway got down on the ivories during his intro to "The Ghetto," the house lit up.

Strange waited with dread for the inevitable comedown of "The First Time Ever I Saw Your Face." Flack had recorded it in '69, but it caught chart fire when Eastwood put it in that movie of his, about the one-night stand gone way wrong. To Strange, it was one of the most lackluster songs ever to hit the charts. But Carmen liked it, so Strange never put it down in her presence. Flack was singing it now, one spotlight on her at the piano. There was a rapt, spiritual expression of attention on Carmen's face.

Strange looked around at the audience. Turning his head back toward the rear rows, he saw a big, rust-colored, misshapen Afro on a light-skinned man, and the large hair of the tall, overly made-up woman who sat beside him.

Strange couldn't believe that any man could be that bold. Still, he wondered.

He put his mouth close to Carmen's ear. "I gotta make a phone call."

"Okay."

Strange produced his wallet and gave Carmen a twenty-dollar bill. "Case I don't come back…"

"What?"

"That's for cab fare. They got taxis out in the lot. I'll meet you back at your crib later on."

"For real, Derek? You gonna *leave* me here?"

"I'm working a case."

"Not tonight you're not."

"I'll explain later on."

"You got plenty to explain," she said.

He had no time to ponder her words. He ignored the looks of reproach from the audience members seated around them and managed to get out of their aisle. Went up the steps between the rows and couldn't help but look over at Jones, who was staring at him straight on. The dude knew no caution and had no fear.

RED JONES had been suffering through that boring-ass song he'd heard on the radio when he saw a man with a thick mustache turn his head and study him from the center rows of the theater. Then watched as the man talked to his woman and got up out of his seat. He locked eyes with him as he walked up the steps. Dude had big shoulders on him and a chest. He looked like some kind of police.

Red Jones turned to Coco. "I smell pig."

"Red, I'm tryin to hear Roberta."

"Let's go."

"For *real*."

"Do I look like I'm playin?"

They got up and took their time moving through the aisle. They were interrupting Flack's dramatic performance and blocking the view of many, but no one had the balls to say a thing.

STRANGE FOUND the pay phone up near the bathrooms. He dialed the Third District house, identified himself as a former police officer, and asked to speak to Vaughn. When told by the desk sergeant that Vaughn was out, Strange left a detailed message and suggested that any available units be sent to the amphitheater. Red Jones and Coco Watkins went past him, taking their time, taking long strides, without a glance in his direction. Strange saw no ring on Coco's hand.

As the two of them went out the gates, Jones stopped to light a cigarette for himself and one for his woman. To Strange, it didn't look like either of them gave a good fuck about being recognized or anything else. But they were leaving, which meant that they knew they'd been made.

Strange watched Jones and Watkins step off the asphalt path and walk directly into the darkness of the woods.

Strange cradled the receiver. He saw a couple of private security guards talking and smoking by the front gates. He walked past them, exited the venue, and began to jog when he hit the lot, where his MC was parked under a light.

NINETEEN

THE CRIME scene at Soul House had been secured by the time Vaughn arrived. Uniformed officers kept witnesses calm and on premises while the lab technicians worked around the body of Roland Williams. Several patrons and the bartender described the killer in detail and the doorman, Antoine Evans, identified him by name.

"You certain it was Jones?" said Vaughn.

"Course I am. Red robbed a card game I was in couple a weeks back."

"Poker?"

"Tonk. But there was real money on the table."

"Where was that?"

"Bottle club, 'round the corner."

"Will you take the stand, Antoine?"

Antoine Evans nodded. "Red ain't had to do Roland like that."

Vaughn found the man with the gray beard, still sitting in

his chair on the sidewalk outside the club, and asked him what he'd observed.

"After the gunshots, tall light-skinned dude came out the House and got back into the Fury he'd come in."

"What was the color of the car?"

"Red-over-white coupe," said the man, pronouncing it "koo-*pay*." "Way those pipes sounded, had to be the GT."

"Can you describe the driver?"

"Shoot, I can tell you her name. Says it right on the Fury's plates. She goes by Coco. Runs a house right here on Fourteenth."

Vaughn had his package for the prosecutors: confirmable details and eyewitnesses who were willing to talk and even testify. Now he needed to make the arrest.

A patrolman approached Vaughn. "Message came over the radio for you, Detective. A citizen spotted Robert Lee Jones at the Carter Barron. We've got units headed over there..."

Vaughn was already moving toward his Monaco, double-parked on the street.

STRANGE GUESSED that Jones and Watkins had left their Fury in the neighborhood of Crestwood, adjacent to Rock Creek Park, surmising correctly that the Plymouth was too radioactive to be parked in the main lot. Their walk in the woods would put them on Colorado Avenue, which branched out to other residential streets. Somewhere on those streets was their car.

Strange got into his Monte Carlo and fired it up. Driving through the lot, he saw two squad cars down by the tennis courts parked nose to ass, the conversation arrangement for uniformed police, but he did not go there for help because he felt there was no time.

He exited the lot and drove west on Colorado. He knew it dead-ended eventually, and it was a bet that Red Jones knew it, too. He would never allow himself to be trapped, so Jones and Watkins had to have left their ride deeper south into Crestwood. He made a left on 17th Street and went down a slope, and as he approached the Blagden Avenue intersection he saw the red Plymouth, doing the limit and heading east on Blagden. Strange hit the left turn signal and fell in behind them.

He stayed as far back as he could without bringing the Chevy to a crawl. Strange thinking, *They don't know my car.* But there was no one between them, and as the Fury neared the red light at 16th and came to a stop, Strange had little choice but to pull up behind them.

He saw Red Jones eye him in the sideview mirror. He saw Red turn his head and say something to his woman, and then he heard the rev of the Plymouth's V-8. Strange brought his seat belt across his lap and clicked in the buckle.

The Fury screamed into the intersection against the red light. It fishtailed and corrected. Strange looked both ways and saw cars approaching from the south.

"Fuck it," said Strange.

They've got brakes, too.

He floored the gas pedal, and the Monte Carlo lifted, leaving twin patches of rubber on the asphalt as it went across 16th to the sounds of angry horns and skidding tires.

Strange saw metal in his side vision but felt no impact, and he thought, I made it; I am on them now.

The Fury made distance on the straightaway. They had more horses than he did, a four-barrel carb, and that Mopar edge, and the woman knew how to drive her car. Strange punched it and felt the wind rushing through the open windows as he gained ground. The Fury dropped down an incline by upper 14th Street, and as he neared the crest, it skidded into a left and he followed. In his rearview he saw a car suddenly coming up from the south at a high rate of speed and he recognized it as a patrol car. Watkins blew the red light at Kennedy and made a soft right back onto Colorado, and Strange followed, going through the stoplight himself, and the cop behind him activated his cherry-top and siren, accelerated sharply, and came up very close to Strange's bumper. When Strange's eyes moved forward, he saw the Fury execute a crazy right, east on Madison, and then the siren whooped behind him. Strange pulled over to the side of the road.

Strange threw the horseshoe shifter into park and got out of the Chevy, his hands raised. The uniformed police officer was now out of his patrol car, moving toward him, his hand on his sidearm, and Strange shouted, "I'm in pursuit of a wanted man," and "I'm MPD!"

"Let's see your badge," said the cop, a young black officer, couldn't have been much more than twenty-one. He drew his .38 and pointed it at Strange.

"I *used* to be a police officer," said Strange, correcting his false claim, the adrenaline gone out of him.

"*Used to* don't mean shit to me," said the cop. "Now turn your ass around. You know what to do."

His father had always told him to answer "Yes, sir" to police, but he couldn't bring himself to say it right about now. Strange placed his hands on the trunk of his car.

"Call Frank Vaughn in Three-D," said Strange. "He'll tell you who I am. Or Lydell Blue. He's a sergeant over in the Fourth."

The cop said nothing as he patted Strange down.

LOU FANELLA had told Gino Gregorio he had to get his own spot for him and his skinny whore, so Gino went down to the desk of the motor lodge and rented another room. When he returned, Cindy and April were snorting lines off a mirror they had taken down from the wall. Gregorio gathered liquor, wine, two plastic cups, and Cindy, and went out the door.

"You wanna be alone with me," said April to Fanella, after Gino and Cindy had gone. She smiled and he saw that one of her front teeth was chipped. "That's sweet."

Fanella knew he'd never relax with Gregorio pounding his pork into some trick in the same room. This wasn't a stud contest. He didn't mind seeing Gino's meat, but not while he was using it.

"Take your shirt off," said Fanella.

Fanella watched April pull her shirt over her head and toss it onto the bed. She had big melons held up in a cream-colored bra and a little roll of baby fat hanging over the waistband of her shorts. Her orange hair was mussed and she hand-brushed it back in place.

April sipped pink wine from a cup and looked around the room. Two double beds, suitcases on the floor, one zipped open showing clothing that had been shoved in haphazardly. A television set was mounted on a metal rack up on the wall, and a clock radio sat on the stand between the beds. Wasn't much here in the way of entertainment.

"Ain't no party without music," said April.

"Put some on, then." Fanella, seated uncomfortably in the room's sole chair, waved a beefy hand toward the clock radio. Bourbon sloshed out of his cup.

April found a Top 40 station and turned up the new Cornelius Brothers and Sister Rose, which had just hit the charts.

" 'Too late to turn back now,' " sang April, " 'I believe I believe I believe I'm falling in loooooove.' "

"Yeah!" said Fanella tiredly.

"Let's get our heads up, big man."

April went to the wood-framed mirror, now laid flat on the dresser, on which she had cut out four more thick rails of coke. She used the clear shell of a Bic pen to hoover up two lines, threw her head back, dipped her fingers in a cup of water, and pinched her nose. The stuff had been heavily stepped on with mannitol, but at seventeen she was a veteran, and it no longer upset her insides.

"Whooo." April held up the pen. "Now you."

Fanella got up out of his seat. His shirt was damp with perspiration, but he did not worry about his heart. At forty he was still strong. He'd heard about coke from the younger guys, how it made your pole like a scratching post for half the night. He thought he'd give it a try.

Fanella snorted a line. As he bent forward to do the second one, he felt April rubbing her boulders on his back.

"Cut it out," he said, but he was grinning. In about a minute he was gonna give her what every girl dreamed of.

"Where you from, Lou?"

"Jersey."

"You down here on vacation?"

"More like a working vacation, honey."

Fanella drew the other line up his nostril. Did that thumb-and-forefinger thing to his nose, like he'd seen the girl do. Immediately, he was in a good mood. Happy. There was a medicine-tasting drip in the back of his throat. He wanted a cigarette and he found one and lit it. He was already thinking about the next one.

Fanella got his drink. He gulped down bourbon and went to the ice bucket and filled his cup and poured another Ten High from the bottle.

A new song had come on the station. April was singing it and strumming an imaginary guitar. "'Sunshine go away today. Don't feel much like daaancin.'"

"Say," said Fanella.

"What?" said April.

"You ever hear of a guy name of Red Jones? Black guy." He was normally careful, didn't run his mouth to whores, but the words were coming fast from his mouth. "I figure, you bein on the street and all..."

"Sure," said April, swaying to the music. She removed her bra and dropped it on the floor. "Everybody's heard of Red."

April pushed her breasts together and winked clumsily at Fanella. Walking toward him in her bare feet, she caught a toe on the carpet, stumbled, and giggled. She leaned in to kiss him, and Fanella put a dry one on her cheek. He wasn't about to kiss her on the mouth.

"You don't know where I can find this Red, do you?" said Fanella.

"Why?"

"I owe him some money."

"I don't have any idea," said April. "But if you give me the money, I'll make sure he gets it."

"You're cute," said Fanella.

April reached out and grabbed his rod through the crotch of his slacks. There was little physical response, and she stepped back and examined his face.

"You all right, good lookin?"

Bullets of sweat had formed on Fanella's forehead, and he'd gone pale. "I don't feel so hot."

"You gotta go to the toilet, right? Number two?"

"Yeah."

"That's the baby laxative in the coke," said April. "Go do your business and feel better, sugar. I'll be waiting for you when you're done."

Fanella crushed out his cigarette, went into the bathroom, and shut the door. She heard air leave his behind, and she heard him say, "Ahhhh," and then groan, "God."

April moved over to the open suitcase and hand-searched it thoroughly. She found a switchblade knife and a revolver underneath some sport shirts. The guy was some kind of hood, so that wasn't a surprise. Two packs of cigarettes in one of the side pockets. And in another compartment, a pretty ring. She put it on her finger and it fit. Probably costume, but that didn't bother her. She loved the way the ring looked on her hand. It was a keeper. He sure wasn't gonna miss it. Leastways not tonight.

April slipped the ring into her shorts pocket, then stripped the shorts off and placed them on the bed under her favorite T-shirt, the one had the glitter star across the front. She stood in the middle of the room in her panties, drinking wine and waiting. Her plan was to get the old man off quick, soon as he came out the head. She knew how, and he would only be good for one. After, she'd wait for Cindy, take a taxi back to Shaw, and get out there and retail her ass like her boyfriend, Romario, expected her to do. There was still plenty of night left.

HAVING COME up empty on Red Jones at the Carter Barron, Vaughn went back to the stationhouse and saw Charles Davis seated at his desk.

"What are you doin here, Charles? I thought you had eyes on Monique Lattimer."

"I did. I was in the playground across from her house for hours. Girl musta slipped out the back of her crib, somethin. I had a patrol cop knock on her door, but there wasn't no one there." Davis shrugged his bearlike shoulders. "Sorry, Hound Dog. She beat me, man."

Muttering under his breath, Vaughn went to the holding cells to take the temperature of Clarence Bowman. He was hoping to put him in the box and see if he could convince him to talk. But Bowman was gone.

Vaughn found Sergeant Bill Herbst out in the office area.

"What the hell happened, Billy?"

"I had to wagon Bowman over to St. Elizabeth's. The guy was eating his own shit, Frank. The rest of 'em were goin nuts back there."

"Bowman's not mental."

"Maybe not. But I didn't know *what* he was gonna do next. Lieutenant Harp told me to get rid of him. Crazy or not, Bowman's gonna be arraigned. Just 'cause he's at St. E's don't mean he's getting off or nothin…"

"I'm not worried about that. I wanted another shot at him, is all." Vaughn rubbed his jaw as he considered the situation. "Let's go back to the jail. I wanna see where you had him."

Vaughn returned to the holding cells with Herbst, who pointed out Bowman's former cage. Vaughn studied the men who had been locked in with him.

They walked back to the office and Vaughn said to Herbst, "Who was the weak tit with the Little Bo-Peep eyes?"

"Henry Arrington."

"Doper?"

"No, Henry takes the Night Train. We bring him in to protect him and let him out in the morning."

"Have someone call me before he gets tossed. All right?"

"Sure thing, Frank."

Vaughn had marked Arrington as prey as soon as he laid eyes on him. He was pretty certain that Bowman had done the same thing.

STRANGE KNOCKED on Carmen's door, a narrow row home off Barry Place that had been cut into two apartments. Hers was on the ground floor.

The house was a wood-shingled affair, fronted by a small stoop more common to Baltimore than D.C.

A cone of yellow light hit the stoop. Carmen opened the door but did not come through the frame. She was still in her dress. A bit of mascara had run down her face.

Strange began to go up the steps. She held up her palm and said, "No."

"Look, I apologize."

"For what?"

"Leaving you like that at the show. Did you have trouble getting home?"

"They had plenty of taxicabs in the lot."

"Bet you had an easier time than I did," said Strange, trying out a smile. He told her about his pursuit of Jones, leaving out the high-speed chase and the chances he took. Said he got pulled over for "barely" running a red and that Lydell had to come to the scene and convince the young police officer not to arrest him.

"You made a mistake," she said.

"Yes," said Strange, knowing they had moved on to something else. He could control some of the damage right now by admitting to his indiscretion. But all he did was lower his eyes.

"Look at me, Derek." He raised his head. Carmen had folded her arms across her chest, and her jaw was set. "You got the smell of a woman on you. Don't you know by now that you can't get that off you? And you have that young-boy's face you get when you know you been wrong."

Strange said nothing.

"Why'd you do it?" said Carmen. "Am I not giving you something you need?"

Strange spread his hands. "Look, I didn't... I'm sayin, it didn't go to where you think it did."

"You mean you didn't fuck her. And I'm supposed to, what, give you credit for that?"

"I'm sorry," said Strange.

"Too many times, Derek."

"Let me come in out this night and talk to you."

"You gonna tell me you learned, right?"

"Please."

"I don't believe you," she said, and stepped back into her apartment. The door closed and the light went off. Strange stood in the darkened street.

A HALF hour later, Strange was in his apartment, sitting in his living room with no lights on, drinking scotch on ice, when the phone rang. Vaughn was on the other end of the line.

They filled each other in on the details of their day. Vaughn told Strange about the beating and robbery of Sylvester Ward, the shooting death of Roland Williams at Soul House, the arrest of the would-be assassin Clarence Bowman. Strange told Vaughn what he had learned about his client, Maybelline Walker, his sighting of the bold Red Jones and his tall, striking woman at the Carter Barron amphitheater, the subsequent chase, and his near arrest.

"That officer did you a favor by pulling you over," said Vaughn. "If you had caught up with Jones, no telling what he might have done. He never even gave Roland Williams a chance."

"Man needs to be got."

"I'm about to take care of that."

"You are, huh?"

"I could use your help."

"I was you, I'd take a whole lot of backup instead. Besides, I don't even have a gun."

"I'll give you one."

"I don't use 'em anymore. Don't even want to touch one."

"You want that ring, though, don't you?"

"Look, I checked out Coco at the concert. If she had it, she would have been wearing it. I reckon it was stolen by those guys who tossed her place."

"Maybe. But there's something else. Four years ago, I walked the extra mile when you needed me. You *know* what I'm talking about."

Vaughn was speaking of their shared secret. April 1968. Strange sipped his drink and looked through his open French doors to the lights of the city spread out below. "Is there a plan?"

"I'll call you first thing in the morning."

"You sayin you know where Red's at."

"Not yet," said Vaughn. "But I will."

TWENTY

LOU FANELLA and Gino Gregorio sat in their black Continental, the morning sun beating down on the roof and heating its leather interior. On 14th, telephone company employees walked in and out of a nondescript building and folks in need of breakfast stood in a line outside a nearby mission. Fanella was smoking a cigarette and sweating into his shirt.

"I feel like shit."

"Those chicks liked to party," said Gregorio. He had not overdone it the night before. He was rested and content, a man who'd had his ashes hauled after a long drought. It did not bother him that he had paid for it. Gregorio had no rap, so much of his physical experience with women and girls, going back to his army days, had been with whores.

"My stomach is still messed up," said Fanella. "We shouldn't have ate that Mexican."

"Quit complaining," said Gregorio. "You got laid, didn't you?"

"Yeah, I got laid. How 'bout you?"

"Cindy? Damn straight."

"Was he good?"

"What do you mean, 'he'?"

"Why not just fuck a boy if that's what you want?"

"I'll fuck you with a baseball bat." Gregorio's acne scars stood out in relief against his reddened face.

"Aw, look at you, you're all mad." Fanella laughed. "I swear you're a homo."

They grew quiet and reflective. Fanella pitched his cigarette out to the street. He looked up at the big windows of Coco Watkins's office and bedroom. He didn't expect to see her. They had already driven around the block and through the alley and had seen no Fury.

"The big lady's not in there," said Gregorio.

"I know it," said Fanella. "But she's gonna want last night's take. I'm betting one of her whores is gonna deliver it right to her. When that happens, we'll find Mr. Jones and our money. Get out of this shithole town and get back to Jersey."

They had gathered their things quickly and checked out of the motel. Fanella had not inspected his suitcase when he had hastily packed it. He didn't know that the ring he'd stolen was gone.

"There's someone," said Gregorio, noticing the figure of a young black woman moving about in Coco's office.

Fanella squinted against the sun. "Could be our girl."

VAUGHN AND Strange sat in the Monaco, idling on the north end of Mount Pleasant Street. The Dodge's recently charged air conditioner blew cool against them. Vaughn was in a light-gray Robert Hall suit; Strange wore bells, a loose-fitting shirt, and suede Pumas in natural.

The block was the commercial strip of the Mount Pleasant neighborhood, and there was much activity. Puerto Ricans, Hungarians, Greeks, blacks, mixed-race couples, and young residents of all types in post-hippie group homes made up the scene. The road still carried streetcar tracks, but the old line was inactive, and buses came through regularly. Henry Arrington had taken a D.C. Transit north on 16th after he had been bounced from lockup. Vaughn and Strange had tailed him as he got off and walked to his destination. Arrington had just stepped into the liquor store near the end of the block.

Vaughn and Strange watched as Arrington, along with a couple of other juicers, waited for F and D to open their doors at ten a.m.

"We gonna go in and get him?" said Strange.

"They got a phone in that place," said Vaughn. "I'm guessing he's gonna buy his bottle and make a call. When he comes out, we'll brace him."

"Little early, isn't it?" said Strange.

"Not for Henry. He likes his breakfast fortified."

"There he goes."

"I was right." Vaughn could see Arrington through the window of the store, talking on the pay phone mounted by the door.

Arrington came out the store cradling a brown paper bag as if he were holding a baby. He looked around, then crossed the street and walked almost directly toward the Monaco. Vaughn got out of the car and leaned his forearms on its roof, waiting. Arrington read him as police and started to beeline, but Vaughn badged him and said, "Stop right there, Henry."

Arrington stopped and stood flat-footed. "Am I in some kind of trouble?"

"Get in the car."

Arrington slid into the backseat. He had the stink of jail on him and the body odor brought on by a summer day. His eyes said he would avoid conflict at any cost. He looked like someone who could be easily taken.

Arrington glanced at Vaughn, who had said his name, then Strange, who had deliberately declined to introduce himself. Arrington would assume that he, too, was MPD.

"What I do, officers?" said Arrington.

"Did you make a phone call in that liquor store?" said Vaughn.

"Yes, sir, I did."

"Who'd you call?"

"I'd rather not answer that question, if you don't mind."

"You don't have a choice," said Vaughn. It was a lie.

"The man in lockup said he'd kill my grandmother if I told you."

"Bowman?"

"Said his name was Clarence."

"And you believed him?"

"Wasn't no upside to *dis*believe."

"How old's your grandmother, Henry?"

"Seventy-eight, somethin like that."

"She'll be dead by the time Bowman comes out of prison." Vaughn looked over the seat at Henry's wasted form. He didn't say it, but Arrington would be dead and buried by then, too.

Arrington's hands twisted at the bag he held.

"Go on," said Vaughn. "Take your medicine."

Arrington unscrewed the bottle top, tilted his head back, and drank deeply. The smell of orange juice and alcohol filled the interior of the car. Tango, thought Strange. When Arrington was done with his swig, he looked more alive than he had before.

"Who'd you call?" said Vaughn. "Say it now. I don't have time to dick-dance around."

Arrington wiped his mouth. "Dude named Red."

"You talked to him?"

"Another dude first, then him."

"Tell us what you said."

"Wasn't all that long a conversation. I said what I was told to say: Bowman failed and got locked up. A man-ho named Martina set him up. And Vaughn is getting close. That's you, right?"

Vaughn nodded. "Now tell me the number you dialed."

Arrington said it and repeated it, and Vaughn told him he could go. Arrington thanked them, got out of the Dodge, and walked down the block.

Vaughn radioed in the digits and asked the dispatcher to get him an address to match. Vaughn and Strange said little to each other as they waited for the information to come back over the speaker. They were both anxious, and somewhat excited, thinking of what was to come.

*   *   *

RED JONES, Coco Watkins, Alfonzo Jefferson, and Monique Lattimer sat in the living room of the house in Burrville, drinking coffee and huffing cigarettes. The men were in slacks and sleeveless white T's, and were barefoot. Monique had a robe on over a bra and panties. The robe was open, and what was visible was provocative. Coco was wearing one of Monique's negligees that she kept at Jefferson's.

Realizing that they had pushed misadventure to the limit, they plotted their next move.

"We gotta leave today, Red," said Coco.

"Your girl gonna deliver us some money?"

"And some other shit, too. Soon as Shay brings me my makeup kit and clothes, we can get gone. I can't go nowhere without my kit."

"You called her?" said Red.

"Yeah."

"And you talked to her about the police stakeout outside your spot?"

"Po-lice lookin for me, not my girls. Shay knows what to do."

"Where y'all fixin to go?" said Jefferson.

"We gonna make our way to West Virginia," said Jones. "I still got people there. You?"

"I don't know," said Jefferson. "Guess I'll head south. Got a cousin down in North Carolina will put me up."

"What about me?" said Monique. Jefferson did not answer her or look her way. He was gonna take her with him but did not feel it wise to give any female too much comfort. Monique was all right; she was steady ass, anyway. But she wasn't all that special. No woman was, to Jefferson.

Jefferson said to Jones, "Give me one of them double-O's, Red."

Jones shook a Kool from the hole he had cut out the bottom of the pack. He tossed it onto the cable spool table and it rolled close to Jefferson. Jefferson gave it a light.

"We about out of cigarettes," said Jones.

"Monique'll go out and get some."

"*Shit*," she said. "Do you know what I been through since yesterday? First I had to talk to that white motherfucker from Homicide. Then last night I had to slip out the back of my spot and not get noticed by that Tom police they put in the playground. Then I had to walk, and get on a D.C. Transit, *and* get a cab . . . and now you want me to go out again?"

"Exactly," said Jefferson. "Get dressed."

"You crippled or somethin?"

"I got two legs and they both work," said Jefferson. "But I'm tellin *you* to go."

"Where your car keys at?"

"Uh-uh," said Jefferson. "My Buick stays out back till I'm ready to leave here. It's too risky to move it now."

Monique looked over at the tall woman wearing her negligee. "Coco, can I take your short?"

Coco dragged on her cigarette and glanced at Jones. On his instructions, they had parked the Fury several blocks away, then walked to Jefferson's house through alleys and backyards. She already knew Red's answer. By way of one, he shook his head.

"Sorry, Nique," said Coco.

"You people expect me to walk? Nearest market's a mile away."

"I was you," said Jefferson, "I'd wear some comfortable shoes."

"Fuck y'all," said Monique. She got up out of her chair abruptly and left the room.

"Where she off to?" said Jones.

"Gone to change her clothes," said Jefferson, tapping ash into a large tray. "So she can get us some cigarettes."

"That woman's unruly."

Jefferson nodded. "She like that in bed, too."

The room fell silent as they smoked pensively. None of them wanted to leave D.C., but they knew it was time to go.

GINA MARIE, Martina Lewis, and the white girls, April and Cindy, were in the diner on U, drinking coffee, having cigarettes, and, as was their custom, recounting the street stories they had gathered the night before. They were in the pre-makeup stage of their day, not yet dressed for work.

"They picked us up in a Lincoln Continental," said April, "and then we went out to their motel room off Kenilworth and had a partaaay."

"That where you got the ring?" said Gina Marie.

"You mean this one?" said April. She put out her hand, bent it at the wrist, and showed the others her new treasure in a way that she imagined a fancy model might do.

"Just tell the story," said Cindy, who knew the details already and was tired of hearing April go on. Cindy dragged on her cigarette, careful not to put the filter to the right side of her mouth. A cold sore festered there.

"So we was doin some nose candy," said April, "me and old Lou, and all a the sudden Lou had to take a shit on account of the cut."

"Thought you said Lou was a professional," said Gina Marie.

"Not with cocaine," said April. "But, yeah, he said he was down here on business. Axed me about Red Jones. Claimed he owed Red money. Like I was gonna talk to a stranger about Red. I be like, I *heard* of him, but I don't know nothin about him." April looked directly at Gina Marie. "Girl, I ain't dumb."

Martina glanced over at April, spent like last week's paycheck. Way her nose was burned up, she could pick either side of it by putting her finger in just one nostril. *Axe. I be. Girl.* April talked blacker than a black girl when she was around Gina Marie.

"More coffee, ladies?" said an employee behind the counter, holding a pot, moving her head to the Fred Wesley that was coming from the juke.

"I'll have more," said Cindy, who was tired out and a little sore. Gino, the blond one with the acne scars, had a pipe on him, and on top of his size he'd been a little rough. He had bruised her some.

"You know that's a fake piece, don't you?" said Gina Marie.

"I don't care," said April. "It's pretty."

Gina Marie flicked ash into a glass tray. "Say what happened."

"While Lou was in the bathroom," said April, "groanin and moanin, I got curious about what was in his suitcase. 'Cause you know I be the curious type…"

"Tell it," said Cindy, losing her patience.

"Well, there were clothes in that suitcase. Also a gun and a knife." April paused dramatically, then put her hand flat on the counter. "And this." The ladies saw a gold body decorated with a Grecian key inlay, one big center stone, and eight smaller stones clustered around it.

"You are one bad bitch," said Gina Marie.

"Girl, who don't know *that*."

Martina Lewis studied the ring.

SHAY GATHERED a cosmetic case the size of a hatbox, and a small red suitcase that held a couple of dresses, slacks, shirts, and undergarments, and some cash, and took the fire escape down to the alley that ran behind the row house on 14th. She went through it and on S she turned right and went over to 14th, glancing down the street at the unmarked police car she had scoped out earlier. The one Coco had said would be there.

The unmarked car did not move. No reason why it would. The man inside it was looking for someone fitting the description of Coco, not Shay. Shay was plainly dressed in jeans and a chambray shirt. She was an attractive female, but in these clothes she did not stand out. It was somewhat unusual for a young woman to be walking in the city with a suitcase and hatbox, but now she was a block north of Coco's house and was among the sidewalk crowd. She went one block farther and at a bus stop waited for a D.C. Transit, and

when it came she got on it and dropped into an empty tur-
quoise seat. An older man who stood with a hand on the top
rail gave her a long look the way men do. Reflexively, she
touched the mole on her face.

The plan was to get off the bus soon as she saw a cab stand
and catch a taxi over to Northeast, where she would deliver
what she was carrying to Coco, holed up in a house in Burrville. Coco had told her she was going away for a while.

Shay was young, no more than a girl, really, and she was a
little bit scared. Her night in jail had convinced her that she
was not cut out for any kind of time in a cage. But things
seemed to be going all right today, so far, and when she had
completed her task...well, she hadn't thought that through
as of yet. She'd do something.

Shay looked out the back window of the bus and with
relief saw that the unmarked police car was not following.
She didn't notice the black Continental that was pulling off
the curb.

TWENTY-ONE

VAUGHN AND Strange crossed the Benning Bridge over the Anacostia River and headed into Far Northeast. At Minnesota Avenue, Vaughn hung a left and drove along a busy commercial strip of overpriced convenience markets, unhealthy food establishments, and an appliance-and-furniture merchant whose profit was not in the sale of household goods but the pushing of credit and high-interest loans.

"These people down here don't have a chance," said Vaughn, with an overly solemn shake of his head. "Course, they *could* try to better themselves. Work a little harder, maybe, so they don't have to live in these neighborhoods."

Strange said nothing. There wasn't any upside to getting into those kinds of discussions with Vaughn.

"Did I say something wrong?" said Vaughn.

"I wasn't even listenin to you, to tell the truth. Guess I got things on my mind."

"Women troubles," said Vaughn. "Am I right? What'd you do, dip your pen in the wrong inkwell?"

"I made a mistake," said Strange.

"Don't beat yourself up about it."

"I should know better. I'm a grown man."

"Exactly: you're a man. It's damn near impossible for a man to be faithful. It's not natural. Humans are the only species who even try. When animals mate, the males move on."

"Men aren't animals," said Strange.

Vaughn's mind flashed back nearly thirty years, to when he'd carried a flamethrower on Okinawa. His nightmares could not even approach the horrific reality of what he'd seen and done. No one, not even Olga, could know the godless dark inside his head.

"Yes, we are," he said.

For a while, they drove up Minnesota Ave in silence. Then Vaughn saw a woman exiting a small city market. She wore a sloppy shift unbuttoned at the neckline, tennis shoes with cutout backs, and held a pack of cigarettes in each of her hands.

Vaughn slowed the Dodge. "Aw, shit. There's my friend Monique Lattimer."

"Who's she?"

"Alfonzo Jefferson's woman."

"We should follow her to his house," said Strange. "Chances are she's headed there."

"We already know where the house is. We *don't* know what we're gonna be up against when we get there. She's a handful, and I don't wanna have to deal with her, too."

Vaughn pulled over to the curb and palmed the transmission arm up into park. He lifted the radio mic from its cradle, keyed it, and called in Monique's description, location, and the direction in which she was headed. He then told the dispatcher to instruct any patrol unit in the vicinity to pick up Monique, arrest her, and take her to the Third District station.

"What're you gonna hang on her?" said Strange.

"Some kind of accessory charge," said Vaughn. "I'll figure out the particulars later on. It'll stick. Jefferson's deuce was used in the Ward robbery, and it's registered in her name."

Vaughn checked his sideview mirror, pulled down on the tree, moved into traffic, and accelerated.

Strange studied Monique's loose she-cat walk as they passed her. "You're about to bust on that girl's day."

"I told her I'd see her around."

SHAY STEPPED off the bus up around the Tivoli Theatre and signaled a taxicab, one of several standing at 14th and Park Road. The driver got out and helped her place her suitcase and cosmetic case in the trunk, then politely opened and held the rear door for her so that she could get in.

"You'd never see that in New York," said Fanella, looking through the windshield of the Lincoln, idling along the curb down by Kenyon.

"*The Final Comedown*," said Gregorio, reading the title of the movie showing on the Tivoli's marquis.

"Never heard of it," said Fanella.

"'The man got down,'" said Gino, reading the copy in smaller letters below the title. "'The brothers were ready.' What's that mean, Lou?"

"Damn if I know." Fanella pointed a finger at the young

folks standing in line for tickets to the matinee. "And I bet none of those rugheads know, either."

Fanella and Gregorio followed the taxi as it went down Irving Street, North Capitol, Michigan Avenue, South Dakota, and Bladensberg Road, then onto a long bridge built over a steady-flowing river. On the busy commercial strip of Minnesota Avenue, they saw a woman bent over the trunk of a D.C. squad car, writhing under the grip of a police officer who was attempting to cuff her. They could hear her cursing the cop with venom and creativity as they drove by.

Fanella and Gregorio laughed.

"THAT'S IT," said Strange, as Vaughn went down one of the high-fifty streets of Burrville, where houses, some run-down and some well kept, sat on large plots of land.

"I see it," said Vaughn, and he kept the Monaco at a steady rate of speed, studying a two-story, asbestos-shingled house as he drove on. He cut a left at the next corner, a single-syllable cross street, and let off the gas, crawling by an alley that ran behind the houses of the block he'd just covered.

"That's the one," said Vaughn.

Strange saw a gold Buick Electra parked in the backyard of the house whose address matched the phone number Henry Arrington had dialed. The yard had a low fence of heavy-gauge chicken wire strung between wood posts.

Vaughn executed a one-eighty in a driveway, turned the Dodge around, and put it along the mouth of the alley. He examined the house. Its second story held bedroom windows, and outside those windows was a gently pitched roof over a screened porch. There was not much of a drop from the roof to the soft yard. A glass-paneled door, accessed by a few iron steps, was situated right beside the porch. If it was a typical house of this type, Vaughn guessed that the door would lead to a kitchen that would open to a living-room area, which would hold steps leading up to the second-floor bedrooms.

"Well?" said Strange.

"They're in there."

"I was you, I'd call it in."

"Not today." Vaughn stared at the house. "You know what a man is, in the end? You know what defines him?"

"I'm guessing you're about to tell me."

"His dick and his work. It's no more complicated than that."

"What's your point?"

"When a guy's equipment doesn't function anymore, it's all over. When he has no job, he has no purpose. There's no reason to get up in the morning. He's done."

"Far as I know, you're still there in the manhood department, Vaughn. And you do your job."

"The white shirts think I fell down on this Jones thing. They think I've lost a step."

"And, what, you're gonna prove 'em wrong?"

"The clock ticks. You get toward the finish line, you realize that what's important is the name you leave behind." Vaughn nodded toward the house. "Red Jones gets it. You don't, because you're still young. But you will."

"I'm not goin in there with you."

"I don't expect you to. Watch the house is all I'm asking. Make sure I don't get blindsided."

Vaughn gave the Dodge gas. He drove across the num-
bered street, turned around at the top of a crest, and drove
back down to the corner so that he could keep an eye on the
front of the house. He curbed the Monaco and killed its
engine. He slid a pack of L&Ms from his jacket, lit a cigarette, and snapped his Zippo shut.

As he exhaled smoke, a taxi pulled up in front of the
house. They watched as an attractive young woman got out
and was handed a couple of pieces of luggage, one medium-
sized and one small, by the driver, who had retrieved them
from the trunk.

"You know her?" said Strange.

"She's in Coco's stable. Goes by Shay. I busted her the
other night."

They saw her head for the house without paying the
driver. The driver got back behind the wheel but did not
leave.

"He's waiting for her," said Strange.

"She's making some kind of a delivery."

"Now'd be a good time to move in, if you're gonna do it.
While they're off guard."

"Let the young lady get out first. She hasn't hurt anyone."

"You're gettin soft."

"Soft." Vaughn grinned. "That's me."

Shay was let into the house through a solid wood door by
a woman they both recognized as Coco Watkins. A few
minutes later, they saw Shay emerge from the house, get
back into the cab, and ride away. From where they sat, neither Vaughn nor Strange could see the black Lincoln that
was parked down the block.

*   *   *

COCO WATKINS carried the suitcase and cosmetic case up the stairs to the bedroom where she and Jones had slept. Jefferson was in the other bedroom, packing a small bag, readying himself to leave.

Coco had dressed in what she had worn to the concert: tight-fit slacks, a silk blouse, and some costume jewelry. Jones, too, had put on what he had been wearing the night before: rust-colored bells, stacks, and the print rayon shirt opened to expose the top of his abdomen. They had both showered, but their clothes were ripe.

Cash was in stacks on top of the bed. So were Jones's Colts. He had cleared the chambers of both .45s, reloaded their magazines, and pushed the mags back into the grips.

"We ready?" said Coco.

"Put the money in that suitcase and we're gone." Jones looked her over. His eyes went to her long-nailed hands. "Where's that ring I got you? Don't you like it?"

"I was wondering when you were gonna notice. The ring got stole, Red. Someone broke into my spot the night I got arrested."

"Was it one of your girls?"

Coco shook her head. "My girls were with me. You're not mad?"

"That ain't on you. It was fake shit, anyway. We get out of here, I'm gonna buy you somethin real."

"You been good to me."

Jones looked at her fondly. "A man's got a stallion like you, he got to take care of it."

Coco chuckled. "A stallion's a boy horse, Red."

"*You* know what I mean." He moved toward the door and brushed his hand across her hip. She felt a tingle up the back of her neck. "Let me talk to Fonzo before we leave out."

Coco unzipped her suitcase and stashed Red's money alongside the cash that Shay had delivered. She found her car keys on the dresser and slipped them into the pocket of her slacks.

VAUGHN SLID his .38 Special out of its clip-on holster, released the cylinder, spun it, checked the load, and snapped the cylinder shut. He reaffixed the rig to the belt line of his trousers, then pulled his right trouser leg up and freed a .45 from the holster that was strapped to his ankle. It was a blue steel, short-barreled semiautomatic, a lightweight Colt Commander. He had found it under the cushion of a sofa in a Southeast apartment a year back, and he had made it his own. Vaughn racked the slide, put a round in the chamber, and slipped the .45 back into the holster on his ankle.

"I'm goin in through the back door," said Vaughn. "When I come out with Red and the rest of them, radio in for a wagon and cars."

"What if I hear shots?"

"I guess that means it went wrong." Vaughn removed his hat and dropped it onto the backseat of the Dodge. "You'll know what to do. You were a police officer. Remember?"

Strange's thoughts went back to '68, when he'd last worn the uniform. In the midst of the riots, he'd lured the man who cut his brother's throat to a place where Vaughn could kill him. That made Strange a murderer, too.

Vaughn got out of the car. He put his right foot up on the

rocker panel and adjusted the leg of his trouser so that it fell cleanly over the holster. He closed the driver's-side door and stepped across the street, not looking either way in the intersection or at the house, keeping his eyes straight ahead to the alley's mouth.

Strange looked at the two-way radio hung beneath the dash.

FANELLA IDLY watched a big middle-aged white man in a gray suit cross the street at the end of the block. They had seen few people since they'd come here, as most of them were at work. The ones they *had* seen were black.

"Who's the old man?" said Gregorio.

"I guess they got whites in this neighborhood, too. Some assholes can't take a hint."

"We ready?"

Fanella glanced at Gregorio. Gino was all right, but he lacked smarts and steel. Fanella didn't want to be wondering where Gino was or what he was doing when the shooting started. Fanella knew *exactly* what to do: go in straight, finish them all quick. Get the money and get gone. Fanella needed no distractions.

"I'll take care of this."

"Just you?"

"I need your eyes out here. Bring the car and pick me up when you hear it start to go down."

"Lou..."

"There's a live thirty-eight under the seat."

Fanella removed the keys from the Lincoln's ignition, opened his door, and went to the rear of the car. Looking around at the lifeless street, he unlocked the trunk and lifted its lid. He found his knee-length white raincoat and put it on. He lifted a Browning 9 mm from under a blanket, released its high-capacity magazine, examined it, palmed the magazine back into the grip, chambered a round, flicked off the safety, and fitted the gun in the waistband of his slacks. He then picked up one of two cut-down pump-action Ithaca 12-gauges that were lying side by side in the bed of the trunk. He broke open a nearby box of steel-shot loads. Working low, he thumbed shells through the ejection port of the shotgun, and when he felt the stop he released the slide and pushed it forward. There would be no time to draw the Ithaca, so he didn't reach for his sling. He held the cut-down under his raincoat, closed the trunk, and walked to the driver's side of the Lincoln. Gregorio had moved across the seat and was now under the wheel.

Fanella dropped the keys into his lap. "This won't take long. Stay awake for once."

"You don't think I can handle this?"

"You don't think?" said Fanella in a high-pitched voice. His bushy eyebrows came together comically as he smiled. "Quit actin like a fuckin girl, Gino. I'll see you in a few."

Gregorio's face reddened as he watched Fanella walk toward the house.

JEFFERSON'S BEDROOM was located in the front of the house. Jones and Coco had taken one of the two bedrooms in the rear. A landing separated the rooms, with a banister running across it that broke open at the top of the stairs. Jones walked down the landing and into Jefferson's room.

Alfonzo Jefferson stood by the bed in his wide-striped bells, synthetic shirt, and two-tone stacks. His woven hat was cocked just so on his small head, and his .38 Special was in his hand. He was winding rubber bands around its grip, held fast with black electrical tape.

Jones looked Jefferson over: dark, slight, and fierce. They'd had a good run.

"You ready?" said Jones.

"Soon as Nique come back with our cigarettes."

"We ain't gonna wait. Me and Coco are about to jet."

"Aw'right, then. I'll see you when I do."

Jones stepped forward. "What it was, motherfucker."

"What it was."

They gave each other skin. And then, from the first floor, they heard someone knocking on the front door.

Jefferson went to the bedroom window and looked down at the yard. His vision was limited. He had no sight line to the stoop.

"Is it your woman?" said Jones.

"Can't be. She got a key."

"Then who the fuck is it?"

"I'll find out."

Jefferson, gun in hand, left the room. As he walked down the stairs, Jones went directly to the other bedroom and found Coco.

"What is it?" she said, reading his face.

Jones looked past her shoulder, through the window to the backyard. She turned her head to follow his gaze and saw what he saw: a white man in a suit, walking toward the back door of the house, his hand on a piece that was holstered on his side.

"Vaughn," said Coco.

Jones lifted his Colts off the bed.

VAUGHN CAUTIOUSLY took the three iron steps up to the paneled-glass door at the rear of the house. Looking through the kitchen to the living room, he saw a small spidery black man in a hat, walking toward the solid wood front door, carrying a gun. He fit the description of Alfonzo Jefferson. Vaughn pulled his .38 from its holster and moved it close to one of four glass panes on the kitchen door.

IN THE Monaco, Strange watched a burly white man in a white raincoat take the walkway up to the asbestos-sided house. Strange had not gotten a good look at the men who had ransacked Coco Watkins's place, but he recognized that coat. As the man got up on the stoop, Strange saw him knock on the door and knock again. He saw him pull a pump-action shotgun from underneath the coat, take a step back, and aim it at the center of the door.

Strange reached for the radio, lifted the mic from its cradle, and keyed it. He called in a Ten Twenty-Four and, without deliberation, opened his door and stepped out of the car.

ALFONZO JEFFERSON heard Red shout, "Hey, Fonzo," but he was already at the front door.

"In a minute," said Jefferson, over his shoulder. He turned his attention back to the door, put his face close to it, and

226 • George Pelecanos

said, "Say what you want." As the last word left his mouth, a great hole blew through the wood. Steel shot peppered Jefferson's neck and lifted his scalp. He tumbled back over the sofa as if thrown by a sudden gust of wind and landed atop the cable spool table.

Fanella kicked the door just below its jamb. It swung free and he stepped into the house.

Fanella saw a figure move back in the kitchen and vanish behind a corner. He went to the little man lying ruined on the table and he pointed the shotgun down at his chest. Fanella kept his finger depressed on the Ithaca's trigger and with his other hand he racked the pump, and as the round cycled into the chamber the cut-down discharged. The body heaved up and blood freckled Fanella's face.

He headed toward the kitchen. Approaching the staircase, he heard movement, and he pointed the shotgun up the stairs and fired, blowing the banister to sticks and splinters, and walked on. He saw the refrigerator door swing open in the kitchen and a man appear over the top of it, and he saw a flash and felt fire. Fanella screamed and pumped the Ithaca, his finger fast on the trigger, and the shotgun roared in his hands.

A BLACK Continental pulled up in front of the house and a lean blond man got out of the driver's side as Strange began to cross the street. The blond man walked toward the house, gun in his hand, and Strange broke into a run. He came in at an angle, and as the man turned at the sound of approaching footsteps, Strange hit him low, putting everything he had into it, wrapping the man with his arms as he had been told to do by every coach he'd ever had, on every football field, and he felt air go out of the blond man and in his side vision he saw the pistol fly from his hand as both of them went to the ground, the man still in his grip. Strange heard a shotgun blast and pops from a handgun as the blond man struggled beneath him, his face both reddening and white with scars. The man was strong, and Strange rolled onto his back. He brought the man on top of him and scissored his legs around his middle and got his right arm locked around the man's neck.

"Stop it!" said Strange desperately. "*Stop.*"

But the man would not stop struggling, and Strange knew he could not hold him much longer. He squeezed his arm tightly around the man's neck.

VAUGHN HAD broken the glass of the back door, put his hand through the space, and let himself into the kitchen as soon as he heard the first shotgun blast. He went directly to the refrigerator, set beside the doorway to the living room, and crouched against it. The old Frigidaire was a left-hinge model, and Vaughn took note of that as he snicked back the hammer of his .38.

The shotgun discharged again. Vaughn heard footsteps coming in his direction, and then he heard the shotgun blast once more. There were no odds in waiting longer, and Vaughn moved off of the refrigerator and opened its door. Now it was a shield in the kitchen doorway, and he came up out of a crouch and leaned over the top of the door and, with one hand on his wrist and the other on the trigger, fired rapidly at the figure in white who had leveled his shotgun in

Vaughn's direction. Vaughn squeezed off four rounds and felt the door punched and a hot sting in his eye, and he turned his head and dropped to the linoleum floor and heard a great ringing in his ears and nothing else.

Vaughn pressed the muzzle of his gun to the floor to steady himself and got to his feet. His face was clammy and wet.

Closing the refrigerator door, his gun arm extended, Vaughn walked with care toward the big man in the white raincoat, who was lying on his back, blood bubbling from two entry wounds in his chest. He was drowning in the fluids filling his lungs. Vaughn kicked the Ithaca across the room. He stood over the man, shot him one more time, and watched death come to his eyes. Standing there in a cloud of smoke, Vaughn dropped the spent .38 to the hardwood floor.

He got down on one knee and slid his Colt from the holster strapped to his ankle. Blood flowed freely down his face, but he did not move to wipe it clean.

This Commander holds seven, thought Vaughn.

He went to the foot of the stairs and stood beside it with his back to the wall. With caution, he peered around the corner, up the stairway at a shredded banister and darkness.

"How's it goin, Red?" said Vaughn.

"Fuck you, Hound Dog."

Vaughn grinned, exposing a row of widely spaced teeth, now pink with blood. "Fuck *you*."

Vaughn heard a dull thud from outside the rear of the house. That would be Coco's feet landing on earth. She was making her escape.

"Where my boy at?" said Jones.

Vaughn looked at the corpse of Jefferson, tangled in the ruin of a blown-up table. "He didn't make it."

"You get the one who killed him?"

"I did him like he did your friend."

The faint wail of sirens reached Vaughn's ears.

"We gonna have to do this some other time, big man," said Jones.

"Don't try it," said Vaughn.

But he heard movement up on the second floor, and then the familiar but heavier sound of Jones landing in the yard at the back of the house.

Vaughn walked unsteadily to the kitchen. Through the open door, he saw Red Jones, a gun in each of his hands, clear the chicken wire fence without touching it, cross the alley, and cleanly leap over a chain-link fence into another backyard. Coco Watkins, holding a red suitcase and a cosmetic case, was waiting for him there. The two of them began to run.

Vaughn went outside, straightened his gun arm, led his target, and aimed. But something was wrong with his sight; the landscape before him was blurred. He put his hand up to his right eye and covered it. He thought this would correct his vision, but it didn't. When he drew his hand back, he saw that it was covered with blood.

Vaughn lowered his gun. "Next time," he said.

Later, an elderly resident of Burrville claimed to have seen a tall young couple running through the backyards of her neighborhood. She said they were moving very quickly and taking long strides. Galloping, almost, and laughing.

*   *   *

VAUGHN WALKED around the house to its front yard. Strange was seated on the government strip, his back against a black Lincoln. He was rubbing his hands together, and his eyes were unfocused. On the ground, several yards away, a young blond man lay on his back, his swollen tongue protruding from his mouth. His face was scarred and gray.

Strange looked up at Vaughn. "You've been shot."

"I'm doin better than those guys in the house." Vaughn pointed his chin at the body. "What happened to him?"

"I didn't mean to do it," said Strange. "I told him to stop struggling...I *told* him. I was tryin to choke him out, the way we got taught at the academy."

"You touch that gun of his?" said Vaughn, pointing to the .38 lying in the grass.

"No."

The sound of the sirens grew near. Vaughn picked up the revolver, fitted it in the right hand of Gregorio's corpse, and studied the marks on his neck.

"I killed him," said Strange in disbelief.

"No, you didn't," said Vaughn, pointing his Colt at Gregorio's throat. "*I* did."

TWENTY-TWO

A WEEK after the violence in Burrville, Vaughn walked east down U Street in the middle of June. He was on leave with pay until the matter could be resolved to the satisfaction of the brass, various city councilmen, and the press.

This is what Vaughn told investigators: he had followed a lead to a Northeast residence where he believed he could obtain information as to the whereabouts of Red Jones and his partner, Alfonzo Jefferson. He did not know that Jones or Jefferson would be in the house. Had he known, he would have gone there with backup. Upon arrival, he found himself in the midst of an armed conflict between Jones and Jefferson and two out-of-town criminals, later identified as contract men employed by the Syndicate. In the violence that ensued, Jefferson was killed and Vaughn was compelled to use lethal force against the hitters from up north. Jones and his lady friend, a notorious madam named Coco Watkins, had escaped. Luckily, a passerby, a former D.C. patrol cop named Derek Strange, heard the gun battle and used a police radio in Vaughn's car to call in an Officer Needs Assistance. Strange, who had taken a bus to Northeast to visit a girl, was walking through the neighborhood at the time and happened to see the two-way mounted under the dash of Vaughn's open-windowed Dodge.

Vaughn's story had holes, and many felt it was bullshit, particularly the bit about the good Samaritan passerby. But Vaughn stuck to it, not wavering in the details, even while he was high on painkillers in the hospital, where he had been operated on for his wound. Vaughn was a former marine who had fought in the Pacific. He was a longtime uniformed officer and Homicide detective with an outstanding record in the MPD. Among the rank and file, he was considered to be somewhat of a folk hero. His injury and his advancing years lent him sympathy. There was little doubt that Vaughn would be absolved of any wrongdoing.

An oppressive heat had descended upon Washington and would remain, with little relief, until the arrival of the first blessedly cool nights of September. Vaughn walked through the sauna, seemingly without care. He wore a new lightweight gray Robert Hall suit and a hat. If he was hot, his discomfort didn't show on his face.

At the Lincoln Theatre box office he bought a ticket. The lady behind the window did a quick double take when she handed him his change. Vaughn had a perforated patch the size of an athletic-supporter cup taped over his right eye.

"Enjoy the show," she said.

"Ma'am," said Vaughn.

He found Martina Lewis in his usual spot, in one of the middle rows of the ice-cool auditorium.

Vaughn dropped down into a seat beside Martina and removed his hat. He glanced up at the screen out of habit. *The Legend of Nigger Charley* had moved over from the Booker T, and he couldn't have cared less.

Martina and Vaughn put their heads close so they would not disturb the others in the audience.

"How's it goin, doll?"

"Frank." Martina's voice was husky. Though he was in drag, he didn't feel the need to female-front to the detective. He looked Vaughn over as the film cut to a daytime Western landscape scene and the light from the screen hit the auditorium. "Nice suit."

"It's new." He had thrown his old gray suit in the trash, as his dry-cleaning man, Billy Caludis at the Arrow on Georgia, had been unable to remove the blood.

"Glad you came by. I was worried about you, honey. Is your eye…"

"It's fine," said Vaughn.

The shotgun blast had stripped a sliver of metal off the Frigidaire and sent it deep into his right cornea. The surgeons had removed the invasive projectile and saved his eye, but the retinal damage had been extensive. In the coming years he would be prescribed glasses, and later a special contact lens, but he would deny the severity of his condition and decline to wear them. For the remainder of his life, Vaughn's right eye could only register shapes and light.

"I called you that day," said Martina.

"I got the message later on."

"Wanted you to know that there was some hitters in town who were lookin for Red. I was afraid y'all would cross paths."

"That's exactly what happened," said Vaughn. "How'd you get the word?"

"White girl name of April had partied with the one named Lou the night before. Lou was asking after Red."

"His name was Lou Fanella."

"Matter of fact, she boosted a ring off him. I saw it myself."

"What did the ring look like?" said Vaughn.

Martina described it. He added, "Costume shit."

"Tell me about April."

"She's trash."

"Know where I can find her?" said Vaughn.

Martina told him that most days April could be seen in the diner next door to the Lincoln, having coffee and smokes before she got out on the stroll. Vaughn thanked him, reached into his jacket, and produced an envelope that was thick with cash. Martina took the envelope, looked inside it, and ran his fingers through the green.

"What's this for?"

"There's a little less than nine hundred dollars in there. It's damn near all I've got in my savings account. It'll get you started, at least. I want you to leave town."

"Why?"

"Clarence Bowman knows you snitched him out. He's in lockup, but that doesn't mean he can't get to you. Red Jones killed Bobby Odum because Bobby talked to me. He'd do the same to you if he got the chance. I don't want that on my conscience, too."

"Isn't your wife gonna be mad when she finds out you cleaned out the bank?"

"She'll be proud of me," said Vaughn.

'Cause I helped out a needy Afro American. Or whatever you call yourselves these days.

Right, Olga?

Martina slowly batted his eyes, his long fake eyelashes fluttering like wings in the light. "I'm gonna miss you, Frank."

"Don't worry, baby. We'll meet down the road."

A little while later, Vaughn walked out of the auditorium. He never saw Martina Lewis again.

AS VAUGHN entered the diner on U in search of April, Strange stepped up to Carmen's house off Barry Place with a bouquet of fresh-cut flowers in his hand. He had phoned her several times over the past week but had been unable to make contact. Strange wanted an opportunity to talk to her, to apologize again, this time from his heart, and to ask for another chance. His pledge would be to prove himself worthy of her love.

He knocked on the door of her unit and there was no response. He thought he might use her outside spigot to wet the flowers and leave the bouquet on her front stoop. If she was on a long shift at the hospital, though, the flowers would be wilted by the time she came home, what with the heat. Better to try calling her again in the evening and give the flowers to someone who would appreciate them.

Strange picked up a couple of fish sandwiches and drove his Monte Carlo over to the house in which he had grown up, on the 700 block of Princeton Place. His mother, Alethea, answered the door in an old housedress and smiled brightly at the sight of her son.

"I brought Cobb's," said Strange, holding up a brown paper bag stained with grease.

They ate in the living room, near his father's old recliner and his console stereo. Strange was silent for most of the meal.

"Everything all right, son?" said Alethea.

"I'm fine."

"Don't lie to me. You never could. Not too well, anyway."

Strange swallowed his last bite and pushed his plate aside. "I been wrong, Mama. I've done some real bad things. Broke every important commandment and some that ain't been wrote yet."

"Only the Lord is without sin."

"I know, but…"

"Pretend you just got born, this minute."

"You mean make a new start."

"Today, Derek. Do something right."

"Yes, ma'am," said Strange.

His mother always did know what to say.

STRANGE HAD gone to his office to check for messages off that new machine he had, but there were none. While he was there, Vaughn phoned him and asked if he wanted to meet for a beer. They had worked together, and Strange had visited him in the hospital, but they had never socialized.

Vaughn caught the hesitance in Strange's voice as surely as if he had read it on his face.

"Trust me," said Vaughn. "It'll be worth your time."

"Okay," said Strange. "But let's do it on *my* turf."

Which is how they came to spend the afternoon at the Experience, Grady Page's place, with the steel-top bar and the posters and funk-rock music, and the mix of police and security guards who were out of uniform, and neighborhood types, and folks burning reefer in the back alley.

"This your spot?" said Vaughn, wearing his suit, hat, and eye patch, seated at the bar beside Strange. Vaughn wasn't the only white person in the place, but he was visibly in the minority.

"You're not uncomfortable, are you?" said Strange.

"I like all the people," said Vaughn, and he held up an empty bottle of Bud so Grady Page, up-picking his massive Afro behind the stick, could see. "One for me and one for my younger brother here, professor."

"You got it," said Page, and Strange was oddly touched.

"What about me?" said Harold Cheek, the off-duty patrolman out of 4-D, seated on the other side of Strange.

"And one for my fellow officer, too," said Vaughn.

Page served the beers. The three men touched brown bottles and drank. Page was playing the *Superfly* soundtrack front to back through the house system, and "Little Child Runnin' Wild" had kicked it off. Strange thought it was one of the most dynamic songs he'd ever heard. To Vaughn it was jungle-jump. But the music didn't bother him. He was with friends and, given his odds at the house in Burrville, happy to be alive.

Even with the music going, they could hear a celebration back by the restrooms, where the security guard Strange and Cheek knew, Frank, was being congratulated by a group of well-wishers that included a couple of comely young women. Frank wore big bells, a wide brown belt, and the horizontal-striped shirts he favored.

"What's goin on back there?" said Vaughn.

"Read this," said Cheek, and he passed the A section of the house *Washington Post* across the bar to Vaughn. "Story about the burglary."

Vaughn looked at the front page. The headline read, "5 Held in Plot to Bug Democrats' Office Here," with the byline of Alfred E. Lewis printed underneath the head. Vaughn scanned the first few paragraphs: five men, most of them Cubans, had been caught trying to bug the offices of the Democratic National Committee on the sixth floor of the Watergate complex on Virginia Avenue. An alert twenty-four-year-old security guard had noticed tape on the lock of a door leading to the garage stairwell, taken it off, seen it reaffixed to the door later on, and notified Metropolitan Police.

"So?" said Vaughn passing the paper back to Cheek. Vaughn had no intention of reading the entire story. There was drinking to do.

"That's Frank Wills," said Cheek, jerking his thumb over his shoulder in the direction of the celebrating young man and his friends. "He's the one who stopped the burglary. Dude's a hero."

"Kinda like you," said Strange, and Vaughn shrugged.

"I didn't exactly succeed," said Vaughn. "My man's in the wind."

"You hear anything?"

"Someone matching Red's description murdered a man in a bar the other night, in a place called Big Stone Gap over in West Virginia. Shot him to death with a forty-five. A witness said the shooter left with a lady tall as he was and got into a taxicab that was waiting out front. It would make sense that Red and Coco would hide that Fury. Also that they would be in that state. Red was born there."

"And?"

"Federal marshals are on it now. I'm done."

"You did your part."

"So did you," said Vaughn, and he saw Strange dip his head. "You all right with it?"

Strange lowered his voice. "I'm getting there."

Vaughn lit a cigarette and pushed the lighter in front of Strange so that he could see the Okinawa inlay on the Zippo's face. "First time I killed a man was on that island. I had him in the sights of my M-One for fifteen minutes before I squeezed the trigger. But I did it. He would have shot me or one of my buddies if he'd had the chance. After that it got easier."

"This isn't war," said Strange.

"Yes, it is," said Vaughn. He reached into his suit pocket, produced something rolled up in a napkin, and handed it to Strange. "Here you go. This'll cheer you up."

Vaughn watched as Strange peeled back the napkin. Inside was a ring: eight small diamonds clustered around a larger diamond, with a gold body holding a Grecian key design.

"How'd you get it?" said Strange.

"I'll tell you in a minute," said Vaughn. "Took a little

arm-twisting, but not much. The girl who had it thought it was a fake."

"I'm not much of a detective, am I?"

"You'll get there, young man." Vaughn looked him over. "What're you gonna do with it?"

Strange stared at the ring in the palm of his hand. "Something right."

"Give Me Your Love" came up on the system, and a couple of young women began to dance. Soon they were joined by two eager young men. Strange and Vaughn drank away the afternoon as the music played on and the folks around them, regal and fly in their natural hairstyles and up-to-the minute fashions, laughed and had big fun. Living the moment in a thrilling, glorious time.

June 18, 1972.

OUTRO

THE AFTERNOON had passed. Leo, the owner and operator of the spot that carried his name, had turned on more lights for the evening trade and kept them dim. Outside, the rain had stopped, and northbound rush hour traffic had commenced on Georgia Avenue. Derek Strange and Nick Stefanos had been here for hours, drinking and talking, and they were relaxed and a little bit drunk. Empty green bottles of Heineken and half-filled shot glasses sat before them on the bar.

The jukebox played "Give Me Your Love," Curtis's trademark guitar and falsetto filling the room. Strange had chosen the song.

"Quite a tale," said Stefanos.

"Just a story," said Strange.

"I've heard some of it over the years, here and there. A few of the details differ from yours."

"It changes, depending on who's tellin it."

"That guy, the heroin dealer with the long nose..."

"Roland Williams."

"I'd heard he was shot in the carryout, House of Soul."

"Maybe he was," said Strange. "I get it confused with Soul House, the bar. My memory could be failing. Then again, damn near forty years have passed."

Stefanos sipped his bourbon. "What'd you do with the ring?"

"I took it back to its rightful owner."

"That make you feel better?"

"The *re*ward did," said Strange. "Dayna Rosen gave me a nice chunk of money. It bought me that sign outside my office."

"The one with the magnifying glass over the letters? How'd you ever come up with such an original design?"

"Funny."

"I'm guessing Maybelline Walker didn't like losing the ring."

"No," said Strange. "But fuck what she didn't like."

"And Carmen? You two patch things up?"

Strange nodded. "We got back together. And then I did the same thing I did to her before. I was just *like* that, Nick. Fact is, I was in my fifties before I got right with one woman."

"You learned."

Strange thought of that Western his father and he used to watch over and over again, where the gunmen save a south-of-the-border village from bandits. "Took me a long time to learn my elbow from a hot rock."

"So where's Carmen now?"

"Carmen's gone. Vaughn, my mother . . . they're all gone."

Strange picked up his glass, examined it, and drank off some Johnnie Walker Black. He put the glass quietly back down on the mahogany.

"What about Red Jones?"

"The marshals caught up with Red and Coco at a Holiday Inn someplace in West Virginia. Desk clerk was one of those police scanner freaks, and he recognized the big man from the description that had gone out over the airwaves. Red and Coco were naked on top the sheets when the law came in with pistols and machine guns."

"They kill 'em?"

"No. I don't recall what happened to Coco. I reckon she did time."

"And Red?"

"Red ended up in the federal joint, in Marion, Illinois. Became the leader of D.C. Blacks, a prison gang got put together to go up against the Aryan Brotherhood and their kind. The D.C. Blacks claimed they were descended from the Moors."

"Yeah?"

"That's their claim. So Red was in Marion. This would be nineteen eighty-two. He got put on the same control unit as his enemies, and some say that was deliberate. That the white guards were in with the Aryans. Right away, Red tried to stab the main AB, and then Red tried to shoot him with a zip gun. This AB, dude had a Jewish name if you can believe it, him and another one of his shamrock buddies, they cut themselves out of an exercise cage with a hacksaw blade and found Red in the showers. To this day you hear people say that Red fought off a dozen men. Truth was, it was only two.

But it was a determined two. When they were done with him, they dragged his body up and down the tier so that everyone could see."

"They made a statement," said Stefanos.

"He'd been stabbed sixty-seven times. Robert Lee Jones was hard to kill."

"And still talked about to this day."

"It's his kind whose names ring out. The others get forgotten. You know what happened to Frank Wills, that young security guard who foiled the Watergate burglary?"

"No."

"He died penniless, in a house with no electricity or running water. By then he'd done a year's time for shoplifting an ink pen. And all those reporters who got famous, all those politicians who made their names on the scandal, all those mother*fuckers* who were doin the dirt, with their million-dollar book deals and radio shows..."

"Relax, Derek."

" 'Haldeman, Ehrlichman, Mitchell and Dean. It follows a pattern if you dig what I mean.' " Strange chuckled, thinking of that old Gil Scott-Heron record he owned long ago. Curtis Mayfield, Donny Hathaway, Isaac Hayes...Gil was gone now, too.

"You better slow down with that scotch," said Stefanos.

"Now I'm gonna take drinkin advice from *you*."

They finished their alcohol quietly and listened with reverence to the music coming from the juke.

"Something bothering me," said Stefanos. "This story you told, those *scenes* with Red and Coco alone in her place,

Vaughn doing his street work, the girls in the diner on U Street..."

"Yeah?"

"You weren't a witness to that. So how do you know what was said and done?"

"I *don't* know, exactly. Some of that shit? I filled in the gaps and made it up. I mean, it's true if I say it is. Print the legend, right?"

"You know that stock boy with the long hair in the Nutty Nathan's stereo store? That was me."

"For real?"

"There was only one stock boy who worked that place in the summer of seventy-two."

"Smartass," said Strange. "Lord, you were silly, even then."

Stefanos smiled. "Let's have another drink, Dad."

"Uh-uh," said Strange. "We gotta earn some money."

They'd been hired by longtime public defender Elaine Clay to gather evidence on a homicide that had occurred in the Washington Highlands area of Southeast. They'd been waiting for the workday to end so that they could interview the mother of the alleged shooter, who by now would be back in her apartment. They were hoping that she could provide a verifiable alibi for her son, one that Clay could take into court. The young man was going to trial in a few weeks.

They left twenty on forty-four. The bald tender scooped the cash up off the bar.

"Leo," said Stefanos.

"*Yasou, patrioti.*"

Strange and Stefanos walked out onto Georgia Avenue. Strange buttoned his leather blazer and nodded toward his black Cadillac, parked on the street.

"Let's go, Greek. The clock ticks."

"What's your hurry?" said Stefanos.

Strange squinted against the dying light. "We've got a case."

If you have enjoyed

What It Was

Don't miss the thrilling new
novel from George Pelecanos

THE CUT

Available now in Orion paperback

ISBN: 978-1-4091-0967-9

ONE

THEY WERE in a second-story office with a bank of windows overlooking D Street at 5th, in a corner row house close to the federal courts. Tom Petersen, big and blond, sat behind his desk, wearing an untucked paisley shirt, jeans, and boots. Spero Lucas, in Carhartt, was in a hard chair set before the desk. Petersen was a criminal defense attorney, private practice. Lucas, one of his investigators.

A black Moleskine notebook the size of a pocket Bible was open in Lucas's hand. He was scribbling something in the book.

"It's all in the documents I'm going to give you," said Petersen with growing impatience. "You don't need to take notes."

"I'd rather," said Lucas.

"I can't tell if you're listening."

"I'm listening. Where'd they boost the Denali?"

"They took it up in Manor Park, on Peabody Street. Near the community garden, across from the radio towers."

"Behind the police station?"

"Right in back of Four-D."

"Pretty bold," said Lucas. "How many boys?"

"Two. Unfortunately, my client, David Hawkins, was the one behind the wheel."

"You just have him?"

"The other one, Duron Gaskins, he's been assigned a PD."

"Duron," said Lucas.

Petersen shrugged. "Like the paint."

"How'd David get so lucky to score a stud like you?"

"I'm representing his father on another matter," said Petersen.

"So this is like a favor."

"A four-hundred-dollar-an-hour favor."

Lucas's back had begun to stiffen. He shifted his weight in his chair. "Give me some details."

Petersen pushed a manila file across the desk. "Here."

"*Talk* to me."

"What do you want to know?"

"How'd they do it, for starters?"

"Steal the vehicle? That was easy. The boys were walking down the street, supposed to be in school, but hey. It's early in the morning, cold as hell. You remember that snap we had back in February? This woman comes out of her apartment, starts her SUV up, and then leaves it running and goes back into the apartment."

"She forget somethin?"

"She was heating up the Denali before she went to work."

"Insurance companies don't like that."

"She left the driver's door unlocked, too. So naturally,

being teenage boys, they got in and took the SUV for a spin."

"*I* would have," said Lucas.

"You *did*, I recall."

"What happened next?"

"From Peabody, David went south on Ninth to Missouri, then drove east. He caught North Capitol along Rock Creek Cemetery and took that cutoff street west, the stretch that goes by the Soldiers' Home."

"That would be Allison," said Lucas, starting to see it, like he was looking down at a detail map. He had a cop's knowledge of D.C. because he was out in it, street level, most of his waking hours. When he didn't have to drive his Cherokee, Lucas rode his bicycle around town. At night he often walked.

"Here's where they got in trouble. David, keep in mind he's fifteen, no significant driving experience far as I know, he loses control of the SUV. Sideswipes a lady in a Buick, which knocks her out of her lane and into a couple of parked cars."

"By now they'd be on Rock Creek Church Road."

"Yeah, there," said Petersen. "The woman in the Buick? Claims she's got neck injuries."

"That's not good."

"I'm gonna work something out with her attorney."

"This kid's father must be flush."

"He is."

"This where the police come in?"

"Happens to be a patrol car, coupla uniforms idling nose out at Second and Varnum see this collision."

"And the chase is on."

"Took the police officer a half minute to put his coffee down and flip on the siren and light bar. By that time, David knew he'd been burned, and he jumps the sidewalk and cuts right onto Upshur Street."

"Driving on the Sidewalk, that's a good one."

"Fleeing and Eluding, Leaving the Scene of an Accident, Auto Theft…"

"Kid's got a rack of problems."

"He fishtails when he hits Upshur. Comes out of that and pins it. You know Upshur going west there —"

"It's long and straight. Downhill."

Petersen leaned forward, getting into it. "This boy is screaming down Upshur, Spero. Blowing four-ways, Wale or whatever coming loud out the windows."

"Nah," said Lucas, chuckling.

"What?"

"Now you're making shit up. You don't know what they were listening to."

"True. They're coming down Upshur, the patrol car, pretty far back but gaining ground, in pursuit. Eventually our boys hit that commercial strip getting down toward Georgia Avenue, at Ninth."

"I know the spot," said Lucas. He was drawing a rough map, very quickly, in his notebook.

"And there's another cop car," said Petersen, "parked right there on the street. The driver is waiting on his partner, who's getting a pack of smokes in a little market they got in that strip."

"What market?" said Lucas.

"I don't know the name of it. Spanish joint, eight hundred

block, north side of Upshur. Beer and wine, pork rinds, like that. It's in the file, along with the address. What happens next is, David sees this police car, and I guess he panics, and here's where he makes the last mistake. He cuts a sharp right into an alley, right before Ninth."

"And?"

"A car is parked in the alley, blocking their way. The boys get out of the vehicle and run; David Hawkins is apprehended on the street. The other boy, Duron, is caught a little while later, attempting to hide in the bathroom of an El Salvadoran restaurant around the corner."

"Who arrested David?"

"The officer waiting in the patrol car. A Clarence Jackson. By then the car in pursuit had arrived on the scene."

"How'd Officer Jackson know that David was one of the boys in the car?"

"In his report, Jackson stated that he observed two boys exit an SUV that they had driven into the alley. Jackson got to David first. The arriving officers arrested Duron in the restaurant."

"Where was Officer Jackson parked when he saw this?"

"It's in the file."

Lucas sat still for a long minute, looking at nothing. He closed his notebook and got up out of his seat. He stood five-foot-eleven, went one eighty-five, had a flat stomach and a good chest and shoulders. His hair was black and he wore it short. His eyes were green, flecked with gold, and frequently unreadable. He was twenty-nine years old.

Petersen watched Lucas stretch. "Sorry. That seat's unforgiving."

"It's these wood floors. The chair sits funny on 'em cause the planks are warped."

"This house goes back to the nineteenth century."

"Your point is what?"

"Ghosts of greatness walk these rooms. I start messing with the floors, I might make them angry."

A young GW law student entered Petersen's office and dropped a large block of papers on his desk. She was dark haired, fully curved, and effortlessly attractive. Tom Petersen's interns looked more or less like younger versions of his knockout wife.

"The Parker briefs," said the woman, whose name was Constance Kelly.

"Thank you," said Petersen. He watched Lucas admire her as she walked away.

Petersen stood and went to the eastern window of his office. Below, on the street, lawyers pulled wheeled briefcases toward the courthouse, uniformed and plainclothes police bullshitted with one another, mothers spoke patiently and angrily with their sons, civil servants took cigarette breaks, and folks of all shapes and colors went in and out of the Potbelly shop on the first floor.

"Life's rich pageant," said Petersen.

"That's a rock record from back in your day, right?"

"Inspector Clouseau, originally."

"You got me on that one."

"I have twenty years on you. At times the perspective is obvious. Other times, no." Petersen looked him over with the respect that men who have not served give to those who have. "You've seen a lot, haven't you?"

"It's been interesting, so far." Lucas slipped his notebook into his jacket and picked up the David Hawkins file off Petersen's desk.

"Bring me something back I can use," said Petersen.

Lucas nodded. "I'll get out there."

THE NEXT morning he stopped by the Glenwood Cemetery in Northeast to see his *baba*. Glenwood was an old but well-kept graveyard, acres of rolling, high-ground land holding plots with headstones memorializing lives going back to the 1800s. His father was buried here, beside his own parents, on the west side of the facility, which bordered dead-end residential streets stemming off North Capitol in a neighborhood called Stronghold. Past this last section of graves the land dropped off and there went Bryant Street, its short block of row homes in a neat descending line. Lucas looked down at his father's marker and placed a dozen roses on his plot. He said a silent prayer of thanks for the granting of life, did his *stavro*, and got back in his four-wheel.

He drove a 2001 Jeep Cherokee, the old boxy model with the legendary in-line 6. The model had been discontinued years ago, but because it was sturdy and reliable there were many of them still on the streets. In that respect it was the aughts version of the old Dodge Dart. With his black Jeep, empty of bumper stickers or decals, and his utilitarian clothing, Lucas was unmemorable by design, a tradesman, maybe, or a meter reader, just another workingman quietly going about his business in the city.

Lucas went up to Peabody and began to drive the route of David Hawkins and his friend Duron. Missouri, North

Capitol, Allison, and then Rock Creek Church, where it had begun to go wrong. He recalled the adrenaline rush he had experienced the day he and a couple of buddies from the wrestling team had stolen a car, back in high school. It didn't matter who suggested it; they had all participated with enthusiasm, and all had been caught, arrested, and charged. They pled down, and, because they were white and came from stable families, they had pulled community service and loose supervision. There were no further problems; Lucas's mistake was a one-shot deal, and he did not want to shame his parents in that way ever again. By the time he entered the Marine Corps, his conviction had been expunged.

He understood why David and Duron had stolen the SUV. Teenage boys did stupid things; their brains were wired for impulse and fun. Wasn't but a little more than ten years back that he had been one of those reckless boys, too, before September 11 and his tour of Iraq. A sobering decade, a decade that stole his youth.

Lucas drove west on Upshur. He gunned the Jeep going down the hill and pulled over when he reached the commercial strip, near Georgia Avenue. He saw the alley, cut along a salmon-colored building, currently unoccupied, where the boys had been trapped. He looked at the south and north sides of the strip and he studied the businesses and the layout of the street. In his notebook he drew a map showing the locations of the establishments. On the south side: a funeral parlor, a dry cleaner's, a carryout featuring Chinese/steak-and-cheese, a nail salon, and a hair salon; on the north side: a storefront church, a market selling wine and beer, a furnishings store that seemed too upscale for the neighborhood, a hair salon, a Caribbean café, the alley, the salmon-colored building, another Chinese/American hybrid, a seafood carryout, a beverage shop, and on the corner a shuttered barbershop. Many of the stores had English and Spanish signage in their windows; there were blacks, Hispanics, and a few whites out on the street.

He got out of the car and, using his iPhone, took photographs of these businesses and their spots on the block. No one questioned him or got in his way. He went around the corner and noted the commercial layout of Ninth: the Petworth station of the U.S. Post Office, a private-detective agency, another funeral home, the Salvadoran restaurant where Duron had tried to hide, an embroidery shop, and a corner Spanish grocery store that did not have any English signage and was padlocked shut. Above the detective agency door was a lightbox that read "Strange Investigations," with several letters enlarged by the magnifying-glass logo placed over them. He had heard tell of the man, Derek Strange, and his latest partner, a middle-aged Greek whose name he could not recall.

Lucas retraced his steps, crossed Upshur and stood by the Chinese eat-house, where in his report Officer Clarence Jackson stated that he had been parked, and saw that indeed it afforded a direct view of the alley. He took a photograph from that perspective. He looked across the street to the market where Jackson's partner had bought his smokes, and he saw that there was a fire hydrant in front of it. That would explain why Jackson had parked across the street. It would have explained it perfectly, except for the fact that Jackson was police.

Lucas crossed Upshur once again and entered the beer and wine market. It was clean, well stocked with alcohol and food packaged in bags, its walls lined with steel shelving and reach-in coolers. Behind the register counter was a man in his forties, round brown face, white shirt open at the neck revealing a gold crucifix in a thicket of black chest hair. By his bearing and the gold-and-diamond ring on his finger, Lucas surmised that he was the owner. When questioned, the man confirmed this. Lucas gave him his name and identified himself simply as an "investigator." He asked if the owner, who called himself Odin, recalled the day of the arrest, and Odin said that he did. He asked Odin where the officer had been parked when his partner had entered the market to buy his smokes, and Odin said, "He park out front." When Lucas noted that there was a fire hydrant out front, Odin, who like many hardworking Hispanics was a law-and-order man, said rather defensively, "But he is police; he park where he want!"

Lucas got the man's contact information, thanked him, and made a note in his book regarding the pronunciation of Odin's name. He left the store and took multiple photographs of the alley from the point of view of the empty parking spot. He framed these so that the fire hydrant was in the foreground of the shots.

THE NEXT day, Lucas was sitting on the edge of Constance the intern's desk, trying to talk her into something, when Petersen called out to him from his office.

"We should continue this conversation later on," said Lucas.

"You think so?" said Constance, a strand of dark hair over

one eye, light freckles across the bridge of her nose. She reminded Lucas of one of those J. Crew girls. There was no trace of a smile on her face, but there was a light in her eyes, and Lucas knew that if he wanted to be in, he was in.

Petersen was behind his desk, loud striped shirt untucked, his blond hair shaggy around his face, looking like an aged Brian Jones. He was checking out photos on his computer screen, displayed from a disk that Lucas had burned from his iPhone.

"These are interesting," said Petersen, Lucas now standing beside him.

"The ones with the hydrant in the foreground? That would approximate the sight line of Officer Jackson. From where he was actually parked, as opposed to where he *said* he was parked."

"He couldn't have seen deep into the alley from there."

"He could only have seen the head of it, and a small piece of it at that. The report says the Denali was found at the back edge of that salmon-colored building. So, from that perspective, there's no way Jackson could have observed David and Duron get out of that SUV."

"Can anyone testify that Jackson was parked in front of the market?"

From his back pocket Lucas produced his notebook and opened it. "The owner. His name is Odin Nolasco." Lucas spelled it and Petersen wrote it down. Lucas said, "It's pronounced Oh-deen. I don't think he'd willingly discredit a police officer's official report. You're going to have to subpoena him. When you get him on the stand you might have to treat him as hostile."

"Thank you for the legal advice, counselor."

"I'm sayin."

"The visual ID, the link of the boys to the SUV, that's the prosecution's case right there."

"Weren't the boys' prints on the Denali?"

"Their prints were all over it. But that's less significant than what we have here. I was weighing a plea, but now I want this to go to trial. You put it into a D.C. jury's head that a police officer gave false testimony to make a case against a juvenile, nine times out of ten that jury's going to acquit, even in the face of damning evidence."

"Well, there's your ammunition." Lucas held up the notebook. "I've got street maps I drew, right in here, if you need them."

"The Book of Luke."

"Yes, sir."

"Good work, man."

"Thank you."

Lucas began to walk from the office, and Petersen stopped him. "Spero?"

"Yeah."

"Don't bother Constance. She's a nice girl."

"I like nice girls," said Lucas. He meant it, too.

IT WENT the way Petersen said it would. A month later, he phoned Lucas and got him on his cell.

"David Hawkins was acquitted," said Petersen.

"Duron?" said Lucas.

"Duron will walk, too."

"Do I get a bonus, somethin?"